The Ghost Dogs
of Whispering Oaks

For what seemed hours, Nancy waited in her hiding place. Suddenly, in the moonless night, four pairs of yellow eyes had materialized over the graves. Nancy edged forward. She had to see these canine ghosts.

Their eyes began roving round and round. A cacohony of chilling sounds now surrounded Nancy. She inched closer and closer, her own eyes glued to the creatures.

Then a cold fear gripped her. Two pairs of eyes had vanished. Nancy whirled around. Snarling, the two creatures now stood directly behind her.

Summoning courage, Nancy turned the powerful beam of her flashlight directly on one of the mysterious creatures. What she saw made her gasp. But at that instant a heavy blow hit her from behind. Nancy crumpled to the ground, unconscious!

Nancy Drew
Mystery Stories

#57   The Triple Hoax
#58   The Flying Saucer Mystery
#59   The Secret in the Old Lace
#60   The Greek Symbol Mystery
#61   The Swami's Ring
#62   The Kachina Doll Mystery
#63   The Twin Dilemma
#64   Captive Witness
#65   Mystery of the Winged Lion
#66   Race Against Time
#67   The Sinister Omen
#68   The Elusive Heiress
#69   Clue in the Ancient Disguise
#70   The Broken Anchor
#71   The Silver Cobweb
#72   The Haunted Carousel
#73   Enemy Match
#74   The Mysterious Image
#75   The Emerald-eyed Cat Mystery
#76   The Eskimo's Secret
#77   The Bluebeard Room
#78   The Phantom of Venice

#79   The Double Horror of Fenley Place
#80   The Case of the Disappearing
      Diamonds
#81   The Mardi Gras Mystery
#82   The Clue in the Camera
#83   The Case of the Vanishing Veil
#84   The Joker's Revenge
#85   The Secret of Shady Glen
#86   The Mystery of Misty Canyon
#87   The Case of the Rising Stars
#88   The Search for Cindy Austin
#89   The Case of the Disappearing Deejay
#90   The Puzzle at Pineview School
#91   The Girl Who Couldn't Remember
#92   The Ghost of Craven Cove
#93   The Case of the Safecracker's Secret
#94   The Picture-Perfect Mystery
#95   The Silent Suspect
#96   The Case of the Photo Finish
#97   The Mystery at Magnolia Mansion
#98   The Haunting of Horse Island
#99   The Secret at Seven Rocks

Available from MINSTREL Books

NANCY DREW®
GHOST STORIES
CAROLYN KEENE

A MINSTREL® BOOK

PUBLISHED BY POCKET BOOKS

New York   London   Toronto   Sydney   Tokyo   Singapore

A Minstrel Book published by
POCKET BOOKS, a division of Simon & Schuster
1230 Avenue of the Americas, New York, NY 10020

ISBN: 0-671-69132-5

First Minstrel Books printing July 1987

10 9 8 7 6 5

Foreword

Dear Fans,

When I thought about creating a collection of ghost stories, I knew that Nancy Drew would face her most intriguing challenge yet as a young detective. You see, Nancy does not believe in ghosts; but the many unexplained happenings in each mystery almost lead her to think otherwise.

Well, I won't spoil the fun by telling you about Nancy's amazing discoveries. You'll have to read the stories to find out what they are!

Carolyn Keene

Contents

The Campus Ghost / 1

The Ghost Dogs of Whispering Oaks / 27

Blackbeard's Skull / 59

The Ghost Jogger / 89

The Curse of the Frog / 107

The Greenhouse Ghost / 133

The Campus Ghost

"**W**e've just seen her, Nancy! The spook that haunts Clermont College!" Plump, blond Bess Marvin was bubbling with excitement.

"Bess insisted that we drive straight back to River Heights and tell you about it, since you're such a super mystery-solver," added Bess's dark-haired cousin, tomboyish George Fayne.

Nancy Drew's blue eyes twinkled. "Tell me the details!" she urged them.

The two girls and their dates had been attending a college dance in nearby Grayton. They told Nancy they had seen the ghost during an intermission while strolling along a wooded creek bordering the campus.

"She was wearing a gray hooded cape, just as she used to when she was alive," Bess related.

The ghost was said to be that of Professor Sophie Hanks, who had once taught science at Clermont College. Five years ago, on a stormy night, her car had

1

gone off the creek road and crashed on the rocky hillside. Professor Hanks had been thrown out of her car into the flooding creek, and she completely disappeared. Since then, a spooky figure resembling the professor had been glimpsed a number of times at night.

"And sometimes a ghostly light is seen flickering in her lab," said George. "I know a couple of students who've seen it. It's really weird!"

After her friends left to return to the dance, Nancy sat watching television for a while. But she could not help thinking of the strange story Bess and George had just told her.

Finally Nancy glanced at her watch, then jumped up from the sofa and said to her pet bull terrier, "It's not eleven yet, Togo. Let's go see for ourselves if the ghost is still lurking on campus!"

Traffic was light and Nancy soon reached Grayton. Circling around town, she drove along the wooded creek road, but no spectre appeared in the moonlight. "Guess we're out of luck, Togo," she said, patting him.

At last she turned toward the college and stopped across from the Science Building. Nancy's heart suddenly flipped. *A faint light could be seen glimmering in a second floor window!*

Nancy hastily started her car again and drove slowly until she sighted a uniformed campus guard.

"You're right, Miss!" he exclaimed when she pointed out the light. "That's the window of Professor Hanks's laboratory!"

Entering the Science Building, they hurried upstairs with Togo running eagerly ahead. When the guard unlocked the door of the lab, they found themselves peering into a totally dark room!

He switched on the light. Test tubes and other items lay on the workbench. They looked as if they had been used recently in some kind of experiment. Yet there were no intruders in the laboratory.

"Looks like someone was just here!" the guard said, scratching his head. "But how'd anyone get in? The labs are locked at night. Students can't get in, and this one hasn't been reassigned to any other professor!"

"There are no marks from a person forcing the door lock either," Nancy declared after examining it.

Next morning at the breakfast table, she told her father, Carson Drew, about the night's adventure. The distinguished lawyer looked startled. "What an odd coincidence! I've just been asked to take on a case involving Professor Hanks."

Mr. Drew related that just before her death, Sophie Hanks had succeeded in making a substance called florium pentose. "It occurs only in rare plants," he added. "Making it artificially in the laboratory was quite a chemical feat."

Sophie had published a report of her work in a scientific journal, but it attracted no attention at the time. "Now, five years later," Carson Drew went on, "my client, the Foster Drug Company, has found an important use for florium pentose. They want to manufacture it by her method. But she left incomplete notes. A crucial property, the catalyst, needed to activate the process is omitted from her formula. And to make matters even more difficult, the process is patented, so the company would have to pay royalties—and she left no heirs. For that matter, she hasn't been declared legally dead yet.

"Still," Mr. Drew continued, "the information is valuable and no good can come of it at all until we find the complete formula. It must be somewhere in her notebooks or records."

With a sigh, he added, "Unfortunately, Professor Hanks's body was never found, so that makes the legal situation even knottier."

"I see what you mean, Dad," Nancy said thoughtfully. "Would you like me to look into the mystery?"

Carson Drew smiled and set down his coffee cup. "I was hoping you'd offer to, honey. If you can come up with any answers, it would certainly be a tremendous help."

After assisting the Drews' housekeeper, Hannah Gruen, in clearing away the breakfast dishes, Nancy drove to Clermont College and interviewed Dean Tapley, head of the science department. He told her a number of interesting details.

Sophie Hanks had been a rather plain, unhappy woman, the dean confided. She had a twisted nose and her face was disfigured by a childhood accident. Even though she was only in her mid-thirties, students called her The Old Witch behind her back.

"I suppose that made Sophie rather sharp-tongued and unpleasant," Dean Tapley reflected, "but we kept her on the faculty, nevertheless, because she was such a brilliant science teacher."

Her papers and records were stored in a locker in the lab. "But we can't turn them over to the Foster Drug Company," the dean went on, "since, among other reasons, she was never declared dead. However, I and other faculty members have glanced through them, and I can assure you they contain no reference to the catalyst she used."

"Did the police drag the creek for her body?" Nancy asked.

"Yes, but she was never found. The storm that night caused the creek to flood, so presumably her body was washed downriver."

The college knew of no surviving relatives. "But a few days ago," he said, "a girl named Alice Durand came here, claiming to be Sophie's niece."

"Is she still in town?"

Dean Tapley frowned. "Yes, I believe she's staying at some hotel. I referred her to Professor Martin. No doubt he'll know which one." Dean Tapley explained that Professor Abel Martin was the nearest to a friend that Sophie had among the faculty. Letters from another friend named Vanessa Lee had also been found among Sophie's belongings, but she had never contacted the college.

The dean directed Nancy to Professor Martin's office. She was surprised to find a young-looking man in his early thirties who taught English literature. He was tall, with rumpled brown hair, and wore a tweed jacket and slacks.

"I know nothing about science." He chuckled. "I guess the main reason Sophie and I became friendly was her appreciation of literature. Everyone was so annoyed by her rudeness, but I got a chance to see that she was just lonely and unhappy; I spent some lovely times with her."

"Did you see her the night of the accident?" Nancy asked.

"Yes." Abel Martin's face suddenly became grave. "To tell the truth, I think she crashed her car deliberately."

Nancy was shocked. He explained that Professor Hanks had just returned from a science convention at which she had read a paper about her florium pentose experiment. She had hoped to win scientific acclaim for this work. Instead, her fellow scientists had shown little interest. Few had attended the session at which she delivered her report, and most of them treated her coldly—partly, Martin suspected, because of her unpleasant manners and appearance.

"She was terribly upset when she got back that evening. She kept complaining that everyone was against her. Apparently she brooded in her lab for several hours, then drove off about midnight at the height of the storm and had her fatal crash."

"Where did Professor Hanks live?" Nancy asked.

"She rented an upstairs apartment in a house near

the campus that's owned by an elderly couple," Martin replied. "When it was cleared out after her death, I agreed to let her personal effects be stored in my garage. They're still in it."

Nancy's eyes lit up with interest. "Then perhaps you've seen those letters from her friend, Vanessa Lee?"

"Yes." Abel Martin smiled reflectively. "It must have been rather a strange friendship."

Nancy was intrigued and said, "Why?"

"Because Vanessa Lee seems so different from Sophie. I suppose they must have known each other since girlhood. Otherwise it's hard to see what they had in common. From her letters, Vanessa sounds like a charming, attractive woman with lots of suitors and a crowded social life." Martin added that although Sophie had not kept the stamped envelopes, the letters had evidently been written from the French Riviera and Mexico and glamorous resorts all around the world. "You can read them, if you like."

"Thanks, that might be helpful." Nancy also asked about Sophie's niece, Alice Durand. Professor Martin said she was staying at the Capitol Hotel and suggested that the three have lunch at the Faculty Club.

Alice turned out to be a slender young woman, not much older than Nancy, with fluffy blond hair and long-lashed green eyes which she kept batting flirtatiously at Abel Martin. She spoke with a sort of cowboyish Southern accent that might have been pleasant except for her whiny voice. On asking where she lived, Nancy learned that she came from Texas.

"How much do you think my aunt's chemical what-chamacallit will be worth?" Alice asked as they lunched on eggs Benedict, which was the Faculty Club's Tuesday special.

"I've no idea," Nancy confessed.

"But I thought your daddy was the lawyer for the drug company that wants it."

"He is. But I doubt if any royalty figure has been arrived at yet." When Nancy added that the amount of profit from making florium pentose depended largely on whether the company could find out what catalyst Sophie used, the blond girl looked irritated and suspicious.

"I never heard anything about that," Alice said crossly. She related that her mother had been Sophie's half-sister, but the family had broken up when the two girls were about eleven or twelve.

"Sophie must not have grown up in the Southwest," Abel remarked. "At least she didn't speak with that kind of regional accent."

"How did you learn that your aunt had been a professor at Clermont College?" Nancy asked Alice.

"I saw a TV news story about the campus ghost," Alice replied. "Then the reporter told how a drug company wanted to buy the rights to some chemical process discovered by this dead lady scientist named Sophie Hanks. I realized she could be my aunt." Her idea was confirmed, Alice said, when she searched her late mother's effects and found a note from Sophie announcing her appointment to the faculty of Clermont College.

Nancy could not help suspecting that Alice had known all along that her aunt taught at Clermont, but had never bothered to get in touch until she learned it might be worthwhile to do so.

"By the way, would you two like me to show you where Sophie lived?" Abel Martin inquired. Alice showed little interest, but Nancy eagerly accepted.

A waiter came to their table. "Excuse me, but is one of you young ladies Miss Drew?" When Nancy nodded, he said someone wished to speak to her on the phone. Her caller was Dean Tapley.

"I hoped you might be lunching there at the club with Professor Martin," he said. "Something has come up which may interest you, Nancy. I've just had a visit from that letter-writing friend of Sophie Hanks, Vanessa Lee. Would you care to meet her?"

"Indeed I would!" Nancy said. He promised to arrange a meeting in half an hour.

Returning to their table, Nancy told Professor Martin and Alice the news. Their visit to Sophie's apartment was put off until three o'clock.

As they were going out through the club lobby, Professor Martin discovered a message for him in his letter pigeonhole. As he read it, a startled expression came over his face.

"Is anything wrong?" Nancy inquired. Without a word, he handed her the message. It said:

9

THIS MAY SOUND VERY ODD, ABEL, BUT I HAVE THE GIFT OF SECOND SIGHT. AS YOU WERE LUNCHING TODAY, I COULD SEE A DISTANT RA- DIANT AURA OVER THE HEAD OF THAT LOVELY REDDISH-HAIRED GIRL AT YOUR TABLE. IN MY OPINION, THIS MEANS SOMEONE FROM THE SPIRIT WORLD IS HOVERING NEAR HER.

The note was unsigned. Nancy looked up in sur- prise. "Who do you suppose wrote this?"

Martin shrugged uncomfortably. "I can't imagine. Perhaps someone on the college's parapsychology staff. They investigate ESP and things like precogni- tion—knowing beforehand about events that are going to happen."

Despite her keen, inquiring mind and healthy skep- ticism about ghosts, Nancy felt a chill race down her spine.

Her meeting with Vanessa Lee took place at the Administration Building. Ms. Lee was a good-looking woman about forty years old. Dean Tapley introduced Nancy to her, then left them alone in a private office.

"Do you live around here?" Nancy asked.

"Up in Harbor City. I'm sorry now that I didn't see Sophie more often while she was alive."

Noticing that the woman had a way of speaking that resembled Alice Durand's, Nancy asked if she came from Texas.

Vanessa Lee smiled. "I lived there at one time. I suppose the accent still lingers." She said that she and

Sophie Hanks had become friends while they were attending a woman's college in New Orleans. "Later, I used to write Sophie quite often, but she seldom answered, so we lost touch."

Strangely, Ms. Lee could not tell Nancy much about her late friend. Looking embarrassed, she explained apologetically that she had suffered a recent loss of memory. "To be honest, I'd forgotten all about Sophie until I read about her ghost in the newspapers. One reason I came here was in the hope that it might stir up my recollections."

Before the meeting was over Nancy also learned that Ms. Lee was unmarried and worked at the Alpha Medical Laboratory in Harbor City.

The pretty teenage sleuth mused about the interview as she drove to keep her three o'clock appointment with Professor Martin and Alice Durand. Although the Lee woman seemed very nice, Nancy could not help feeling there was something rather secretive and mysterious about her.

Sophie's former address in Grayton proved to be a modest frame house in a wooded area on the outskirts of town, not far from the college. Abel Martin and Alice were waiting in his car as Nancy drove up.

A sweet-faced woman answered when Abel rang the doorbell. He introduced the woman and her husband as Mr. and Mrs. Bascomb. "Our upstairs apartment is empty again," she said. "Our last tenant moved out last week, at the end of the spring term, so you're free to look at it, if you like."

The rooms and furnishings were old-fashioned, but looked clean and comfortable. Nancy scanned each room with sharp-eyed interest, wondering if one might still hold Sophie's scientific secret.

"Was the apartment ever searched after her things were cleared out?" Nancy asked.

"Well, not exactly searched," said Mr. Bascomb, "but the walls were painted, and the carpet and furniture were all cleaned spic and span. I guarantee nothing got left behind. To tell the truth, we didn't have much to do with Professor Hanks. She kept to herself most of the time."

When the three left the house, Abel said to Nancy, "If you're wondering whether Sophie left any notes about that catalyst among her belongings in my garage, the answer is no. I've been all through them." He added thoughtfully, "She did all her scientific work on campus. At home, after hours, she seemed to put all that out of her mind."

Returning to her car, Nancy noticed that it was four o'clock. She stopped in a drugstore to make a long-distance phone call to the Alpha Medical Laboratory and then drove to Harbor City.

Even though it was past closing time, the lab director had promised to wait for her. He was a tall, spare man wearing rimless pinch-nose glasses. Though willing to be helpful, he was unable to tell Nancy much beyond the fact that Vanessa Lee was employed there as a laboratory technician.

"How much do you know about Ms. Lee's background?" Nancy asked.

"Almost nothing. We employed her on the recommendation of Dr. Norman Craig of New York City. And I must say, we've never regretted doing so. She's an excellent worker—quiet and very dependable."

Nancy questioned him further, but learned nothing important. One aspect puzzled her as she drove home to River Heights. From her letters as described by Professor Martin, Vanessa Lee sounded rich and well-traveled. Yet she was now working quietly in a rather humble laboratory job.

Hannah Gruen had kept a roast beef dinner warm for Nancy. The teenage sleuth had barely finished eating when the phone rang. It was Abel Martin.

"A thought just occurred to me," he said. "There's an old shack in the woods near Sophie's apartment. She used to go there and write poetry."

"Poetry?" Nancy exclaimed in surprise.

Martin chuckled. "Sounds eccentric, I know, but Sophie had a strange romantic side to her nature that the rest of the faculty knew nothing about. When I told you she did all her scientific work on campus, I guess that's what reminded me of the shack. So far as I know, it's never been searched. Would you care to check it out with me?"

Nancy eagerly accepted, and he promised to pick her up in twenty minutes. Darkness had fallen, and a shimmering gold moon was veiled behind misty clouds as Nancy and Professor Martin walked through the woods toward the old cabin.

"Who owns it?" Nancy asked.

"No one. It's been empty and abandoned ever since

13

I came to Grayton. Sophie used to bring a deck chair and portable lamp out here on summer evenings, to read and write."

Suddenly Nancy stopped with a gasp and laid a hand on Abel's arm. "Look!" she whispered.

A pale figure had just appeared among the trees a short distance ahead. *It was wearing a hooded cape, as Sophie's ghost was said to do!*

Nancy could feel goose bumps rising on her skin as she recalled the unsigned message at the Faculty Club—"*this means someone from the spirit world is hovering near her!*"

The spectre seemed to sense their presence. It turned its head—just long enough for Nancy to glimpse a ghastly white witchlike face!

The next instant, the pale figure flitted off among the clustering trees.

"Come on!" Nancy urged. "Let's go after it!"

As she started forward, Abel Martin followed, but a few paces further on, he tripped in the tangled underbrush. Instinctively he grabbed Nancy's arm for support. Both lost their balance and fell!

Nancy scrambled to her feet and switched on the flashlight she had brought from her car. She played the beam back and forth through the trees but failed to catch any glimpse of the pale, caped figure. The spectre had disappeared!

Nancy murmured her disappointment. "Never mind," she said to her companion. "Let's go look in the cabin."

The old shack was dank and empty. Glass was missing from one of the two windows, and the other pane was cracked. Rain had leaked in through a hole in the roof. The only furnishings were a rickety table and rusty stove.

Suddenly Nancy's eyes fell on a boxlike object in one corner of the room. It was an old metal milk chest. Lifting the lid, she gave a little cry of excitement. Inside were several papers!

All but one bore poems in a woman's handwriting. *The last sheet was a typewritten will, signed by Sophie Hanks!* Nancy read it hastily and announced, "It says that she leaves everything to her beloved niece, Alice Durand!"

Abel Martin took the will and glanced at its contents, then looked up with a low whistle. "Quite a break for Alice!"

"Yes, isn't it?" Nancy agreed. "Shall I turn this over to my father?"

The literature professor nodded with a slightly dazed expression. "I guess that would be wisest."

When Nancy arrived home, Carson Drew scrutinized the document with keen interest. "It may take a while to determine if this is valid," he said.

"Yes. I think it should be examined carefully, so that we can be sure," Nancy urged.

Before they could discuss the matter further, Bess Marvin and George Fayne dropped in. The two girls listened wide-eyed as Nancy described the weird figure she and Professor Martin had seen.

"Hypers!" said George. "That ghost really gets around!"

"Ooh, I think I may have nightmares tonight!" Bess squeaked nervously.

The scary episode had given Nancy an idea. "How would you two like to do a little private-eyeing for me tomorrow?" she proposed.

The cousins excitedly agreed to do so. Nancy asked them to shadow Alice Durand. Then she called the house detective at the Capitol Hotel, who was a friend of the Drews, and asked him to assist the two amateur sleuths in any way possible.

The next day Nancy drove back to Clermont College and looked up the campus guard who had gone with her to investigate the glimmering light in Professor Hanks's former laboratory. "We know the door leading into the lab from the corridor was locked," she said. "Is there any other way into or out of the lab?"

The guard frowned thoughtfully and pushed back his cap before replying. "Well, actually, yes. There's a small door in the lab's storage closet that leads down to a cellar. But it hasn't been used in years because those stairs are rickety and have no railing, so it's always kept latched."

"Was it latched Monday night?" Nancy asked.

"You bet!" He nodded firmly. "I put some things away in the closet before locking up that evening, and I noticed then that it was latched."

"Could we check again?" she persisted.

Reluctantly he accompanied her to the Science Building. To his amazement, the closet door in the laboratory was now *unlatched!*

"I still say it was locked Monday night," the guard declared. "No one could've gotten in this way!"

Nancy smiled. "Maybe not. But whoever caused that glimmering light we saw," she pointed out, "could have gotten out this way."

And that person, she reflected privately, must also have been someone who knew the lab well enough to be aware of that closet door!

Using a public telephone in the Administration Building, Nancy placed a call to Dr. Norman Craig in New York. His answering service informed her, after Nancy identified herself and stressed the urgency of her call, that Dr. Craig was out of town but might be reached at the marina in Harbor City.

The girl detective was soon on her way there. Much to her disappointment, on arriving at the marina, Nancy learned that Dr. Craig was out on the bay in his cabin cruiser but was expected back that afternoon.

Nancy lunched on a hamburger and milkshake at the marina diner. Then she waited patiently for the physician to return. It was past three o'clock when his cruiser finally nosed into its slip. Luckily he recognized Nancy's name at once and willingly answered her questions.

She explained that she was investigating the campus ghost mystery at Clermont College and was checking into the background of Vanessa Lee. "Her

17

employer says you recommended her," Nancy concluded. "Do you mind telling me how that happened?"

"Not at all," Dr. Craig replied. "I rescued Ms. Lee at sea, following a boating accident. She was the only survivor of the yacht *Esmeralda,* which foundered during a storm."

He then went on to relate that his cabin cruiser had picked up Vanessa from one of the yacht's lifeboats. The shock of her ordeal had caused a complete loss of memory, and she was hospitalized for months.

"At first," the doctor went on, "she kept mumbling the words *Brahma cattle.* That plus her accent later on, when she was able to speak more clearly, suggested that she might have come from Texas or the cattle-raising region of the Southwest."

"Couldn't you have found out who she was from the yacht's owner or his family?" Nancy asked.

Dr. Craig shook his head. "No, they all went down with the *Esmeralda,* and there was no passenger list available. But gradually part of her memory returned, and she was able to tell us who she was."

The yacht, he added, had reportedly been bound on a round-the-world cruise. Presumably all Vanessa's clothes and belongings were aboard. Since she was thus left without any resources, he had recommended her for a job at the Alpha Medical Laboratory.

At dinner that evening, Nancy told her father about Vanessa Lee's harrowing experience, and how Dr. Norman Craig had rescued her and helped her begin a new life.

Carson Drew nodded. "I'm not surprised. Dr. Craig is famous for his many acts of kindness."

"Do you know him, Dad?"

"Only by reputation. He's one of the most skilled plastic surgeons in the East."

"*Plastic* surgeon?" Nancy echoed, her eyes widening.

"Yes, why? Is that important?"

"I'm not sure . . . It may be." After musing quietly for a few minutes, Nancy telephoned the doctor's residence in New York. She and the surgeon talked for many minutes.

She was just hanging up when Bess arrived to report on her day's activities as a private eye. The information she related was as exciting to Nancy as it was to her plump, blond friend. Bess ended by saying that Alice Durand had gone to visit Professor Martin, and that George was keeping watch on his house.

"Wonderful!" Nancy exclaimed. "Let's go and check with her right now!"

"Well . . . all right." With a piteous glance, Bess added, "But couldn't I have just a quick bite to eat first? Honestly, Nancy, I'm starving!"

Nancy giggled. "Okay, but only three hundred calories!"

The two girls were soon driving toward Grayton in Nancy's car. They found slim, dark-haired George Fayne lurking in a shadowy clump of shrubbery across from Abel Martin's house.

"Is Alice still over there?" Nancy queried.

19

"She is unless she sneaked out the back door."

"Great. Then here's what I'm going to do." Nancy spoke quickly. She handed George some sandwiches and other goodies that Hannah Gruen had packed while Bess was eating. "Here's something to munch on in the meantime."

George hugged her friend and greedily opened the paper bag. "You're a life-saver!"

Leaving the two cousins, Nancy crossed the street alone and rang the bell. Abel Martin came to the door. He seemed embarrassed to discover that his caller was Nancy Drew. "I . . . er, I'm rather busy this evening," he mumbled.

"That's all right. I won't stay long," Nancy said with a bright smile, edging her way inside.

Alice Durand was seated in the living room. She was obviously no more pleased than her host at Nancy Drew's unexpected arrival. "Since you're here," she said sourly, "you can tell me how long it'll take to validate that will you found last night."

"Probably several days," Nancy said. "Dad has turned it over to the court. It will have to be examined by experts on questionable documents."

Alice and Martin exchanged quick frowning glances. Then Nancy asked casually if she could use his typewriter for a few minutes, saying she wished to leave a brief report of her investigation at the college office, but had neglected to write it out before leaving River Heights.

"Help yourself," Abel Martin said curtly. He jerked

a thumb toward his study and workroom at the right of the vestibule. Nancy had already glimpsed his desk and typewriter there.

"May I borrow a piece of paper too, please?"

"Be my guest."

After typing for several moments, Nancy emerged to rejoin the couple in the living room.

"Don't let us keep you, if you have to get over to the college," Alice said with an acid smile.

Nancy smiled back apologetically. "I hope you'll forgive me, but I'm afraid I fibbed a bit."

"Fibbed? What about?" Martin demanded.

"Using your typewriter. For one thing, I wondered if you'd object. I also wanted a sample from your machine to compare with the typing of that will."

"*What!*" Professor Martin glared at Nancy, and Alice sprang from her chair. "Are you accusing us of faking that will?"

"Not yet," said Nancy. "But I must warn you you're both under suspicion. The chambermaid who straightened up your room this morning, Miss Durand, found a gray hooded cape there, and a white-faced Halloween witch's mask."

Martin and Alice burst into loud, angry protests. But Nancy was no longer listening. Through the window, she had just seen a light glimmering on the second floor of the darkened Science Building, a block away on the college campus!

"Please excuse my hasty exit," Nancy interrupted the two. "I have to get over to the college—immediately!"

As Martin and Alice stared in amazement, she dashed out of the house and across the street to her two friends. "Come on!" she cried to Bess and George. "I think the campus ghost is back!"

Piling into the car, they sped toward the college, picking up the guard at the gate. Nancy parked near the Science Building, and they hurried inside.

As they ran upstairs to the second floor, they heard a loud explosion! In the laboratory they found Vanessa Lee lying on the floor unconscious, her face smudged, but otherwise apparently unhurt. Over her dress she had on a ripped gray cape!

The room was lit only by the flame of a Bunsen burner. On the workbench lay the shattered remains of some chemical apparatus that had evidently blown up during an experiment. Luckily, judging by the marks on the ceiling, most of the force of the blast seemed to have been directed upward.

As the guard switched on the overhead fluorescent lights, the three girls anxiously revived the victim. The pleasant-faced woman looked around with a dazed expression as she regained consciousness. The girls helped her into a comfortable armed desk chair at one end of the laboratory.

"What on earth are all you people doing here?" she murmured.

"I'll explain in a moment," Nancy said. "But, first, are you sure you're all right, Professor Hanks?"

"Quite all right, thank you."

Bess, George, and the guard stared in open-mouthed amazement. "Wh-Wh-What do you mean

'Professor Hanks'?" the guard stuttered. "She's dead!"

"A temporary ghost maybe," Nancy responded with a smile, "but definitely not dead!"

She explained that on the night of the accident, Sophie had fallen into the creek and been swept out to the bay. "Several craft were wrecked in the storm that night," she added, "and I suspect that's how Professor Hanks happened to wind up in one of the *Esmeralda's* lifeboats."

Sophie-alias-Vanessa was listening intently, her fingers pressed to her temples, and now she nodded. "Yes, it's all coming back to me. I was struggling desperately to stay afloat, clinging to some debris. Then I saw this empty lifeboat and managed to pull myself aboard."

Nancy went on. "Her face had been badly cut during the car crash. That, plus the terrible disappointment she suffered at the science convention, and the shock of almost drowning, caused her to lose her memory. Dr. Craig, who rescued her in his cruiser, not only treated her cuts—he also repaired the facial injuries she had received in a childhood accident. But even though her natural attractive looks were restored, she still hadn't really regained her memory."

Vanessa Lee, Nancy conjectured, was just a figment of Sophie's imagination—the kind of person she desperately longed to be. "Besides composing poetry, she also made up those letters to herself. As Vanessa, she also spoke with the accent she had had long ago as a happy little girl in Texas."

Sophie Hanks confirmed Nancy's guess. Deeply

23

troubled by her loss of memory, from time to time she would undergo emotional blackouts. On such occasions, she would return to Clermont College—like a sleepwalker or a person in a trance—struggling to recall her past and wearing the same kind of cape she used to wear when teaching there. Her keys, which had still been in her pocket when she was rescued at sea, enabled her to open any locked doors.

"Then I'd come to again as Vanessa Lee," she explained, "and find myself on campus or in this lab, but have no idea how I got here."

"I suppose that, deep down, you never *wanted* to be Professor Hanks again," said Nancy, "because her life had been so unhappy." With a twinkle she added, "But I'm sure you have a wonderful career ahead, now that you're about to become a rich and famous scientist—with a drug company paying for permission to use your great discovery! We should really celebrate this explosion," Nancy added. "You might never have been jolted out of your memory loss without it!"

Then she smiled. "And now Professor Martin and good old Alice will get what they deserve."

"What about that missing scientific bit—the catalyst?" asked George Fayne. "Can you remember that too?"

Professor Hanks smiled. "No problem. I never forgot. It's the bromate. I was trying to repeat my experiment tonight—and it worked so terrifically, I almost blew myself up!"

Nancy pointed to a spilled chemical container that

had been knocked off the workbench by the blast. It was labeled *Potassium Bromate*.

"When Dr. Craig rescued her, he thought she was mumbling *Brahma cattle*. I'll bet that what she was actually trying to say," Nancy explained with a chuckle, "was *bromate catalyst!*"

Without warning, Dr. Hanks threw her arms around Nancy. "You are amazing!" she exclaimed. "How can I ever repay you for restoring me to myself?"

The Ghost Dogs of Whispering Oaks

Strong winds spattered the windshield of Nancy's car with autumn leaves. The girl detective fought to steady her swaying convertible.

"Wow! Some wind!" said George Fayne, a close girlfriend, who was in the rear seat with her cousin Bess Marvin.

George said to a pretty companion beside Nancy, "Sally, do you really mean that none of your family has ever dared stay all night at Whispering Oaks?"

Sally McDonald Butler glanced uneasily at the thrashing trees and continued her story. She was a childhood friend of Nancy's, and desperately needed her help to solve the mystery surrounding a farm owned by her family.

"Since the death of my great-grandparents who built the house, no one has ever stayed there after dusk."

She nervously fingered her long dark hair.

"What is everyone afraid of?" George persisted. Sally looked at her carefully, as if to see if she could be trusted.

"The farm is haunted by ghost dogs!" she finally blurted out.

George's eyes widened, while Bess started. Nancy already knew part of the story, so she gave her full attention to the difficult driving.

"Why do you want to go there?" Bess asked, bewildered.

"I saw the farm only once when I was younger— and I fell in love with it," Sally explained dreamily. "I wish my husband, Jeff, and I could live there. But first," she added, determination in her voice, "I must see for myself if the story of the horrible dogs is true."

Bess stared out the window. Persistent wind lashed the trees. She shivered at the thought of the haunted farmhouse ahead.

"Look out!" she screamed suddenly.

With a tremendous crack an enormous tree came hurtling toward the girls!

The car leaped forward. Nancy had already floored the accelerator. The great oak crashed to the ground, inches behind the car. Nancy braked and turned to her white-faced companions.

"That was close," George said shakily as the girls eyed the massive trunk.

"It's a warning!" Sally whispered hoarsely. She seemed strangely unnerved.

"The wind blew it over," Nancy insisted, trying to

calm her, but Sally seemed unconvinced. She warily eyed the swaying branches.

"Let's go see why it fell," Nancy suggested.

As the girls got out of the car, the sharp breeze whipped their hair. Slender and athletic George was first to reach the base of the tree.

"Look!" she cried. "The tree was cut down!" The others rushed forward.

Nancy knelt to look. "Somebody deliberately chopped this tree so that it would fall on us," the young detective announced grimly. "The cuts are still fresh."

"Not someone!" Sally shrieked. "The ghosts! We mustn't go on!" Tears welled in her eyes.

"Let's go back to the car," said Nancy gently, putting an arm around her friend. She realized how much courage it had taken for Sally even to attempt the journey. Now the strain was beginning to show.

Inside the car, Nancy smoothed her strawberry-blond hair. "It's impossible to go back," she stated. "The road behind us is blocked completely. The way ahead leads directly to the farm." She looked at Sally. "And, spooks or no spooks, I want to know why someone tried to stop us from reaching the house."

"So do we!" cried Bess and George.

Sally managed a nervous smile.

"Then on to Whispering Oaks," declared Nancy, starting off.

"Those ghostly dogs had better beware," George said with a grin. "Nancy Drew is coming!"

29

They rode on for less than a mile. "There it is!" Bess cried excitedly.

Through dense oak trees an old stone farmhouse came into view. Two chimneys flanked the two-story building. White painted trimwork made a becoming contrast to the gray stone.

"It's just as I remember it!" Sally cried with delight. "That igloo-shaped building through the trees to the right is the spooky ice house. The hill to the left was my favorite place for rolling down that time I visited." She giggled. "Oh, and you can barely see the lake beyond the house."

"It's enchanting," Nancy murmured.

Sally leaned forward excitedly as they drew close. Suddenly her face fell. The others, too, stared in dismay.

Everywhere the grounds were overgrown. Shutters hung crazily from broken hinges. The paintwork was peeling badly.

"The barn!" cried Sally, horrified. The others observed the charred remains through the trees. "The farm looks almost evil now," Sally choked through tears. Everywhere, the atmosphere was one of decay and neglect.

"Let's go inside," suggested Nancy as she pulled up to the front door. The girls unloaded the car and went inside. The floor boards creaked as the visitors entered the living room.

"Ugh!" George exclaimed, picking a hanging cobweb from her short dark hair.

The girls surveyed the room. Yellowed sheets covered the furniture. Thick dust lay everywhere. Outside, the wind howled. Loose shutters rattled and beat against the house.

"It's no better in here," George declared.

"This place is spooky," Bess said and shivered. The room was chilly.

"I think it's lovely," Nancy protested. "Although it does need a little housework," she admitted.

"A little?" Sally laughed quietly.

Nancy grinned. It was good to see her friend smile. "Well, at least we can make it more livable."

The girls opened the supplies they had purchased along the way at the general store.

"George, why don't you make a fire," Nancy suggested.

She herself filled and lit the kerosene lamps. Handing one to Bess, she said, "You can put the food away and start supper, while Sally and I uncover the furniture."

"My favorite room: the kitchen. Just lead me to it," Bess joked, and Sally directed her through a door on their left.

"What's behind the other door?" George questioned.

"The library. My great-grandparents loved to read."

Despite frequent sneezes, the girls soon completed their job. They all agreed that the work had brought a cheerful change.

"I'm sorry the house is so primitive," Sally said, as

they warmed themselves before the fire. "There's no electricity or telephone. Even the kitchen stove is wood-burning."

"Speaking of stoves," Bess said hopefully, "I'm starving!"

In no time, they were busy eating a delicious meal of lamb chops with mint sauce, mashed potatoes, and string beans. George tutted disapprovingly as her blond cousin reached for a second helping of apple crisp. Bess, who ignored her, tended to be slightly plump.

Dishes clean, the girls settled before the fireplace.

"Tell us about the farm and its ghostly canines," Nancy coaxed.

Sally glanced outside uneasily at the darkening sky and began. "It was my father's grandparents, Ezra and Pollyanna McDonald, who lived here. They loved the solitary beauty of the mountains." Sally sighed. It was a love she plainly shared. "The farm was alive then with horses, cows, chickens, cats, and goats." She giggled. "The McDonalds kept a large flower and vegetable garden. I believe their pet goat once tried to eat half of it—non-stop!"

Her companions grinned, but Sally's face clouded. "The McDonalds also raised black Labrador retrievers. A year before the couple died, a female dog whelped four unusually large males."

"What does that mean?" Bess asked.

"To whelp is to give birth," Sally explained. "The four dogs became the McDonalds' constant companions. They ruled Whispering Oaks. No one ever entered the farm without the dogs' approval."

"What happened to them after the McDonalds' deaths?" Nancy asked.

"The dogs were brokenhearted. They refused to eat. Tragically, they died one after the other." The girls were moved with sadness. "Trass Sabuch, who looked after the farm, buried them behind the ice house."

Nancy leaned forward. "Are they the dogs that haunt Whispering Oaks?"

Sally nodded and took a long breath. "It was months before the McDonald will could be read. When it was," she continued with emotion, "it contained their fondest wish. They wanted their beloved dogs buried with them on the hill."

Nancy frowned. "Then the dogs were buried in the wrong place?"

"Yes!" Sally cried. "That's why they haunt us. We followed the rest of the will. Four specifically inscribed headstones were placed over each grave, but it was too late."

"Why did it take so long to read the will?" questioned the young detective.

"Because it was missing for a while," Sally responded. "And there's something else that's still missing, too. The McDonalds had exact images of each of the dogs cast in four-inch-high solid gold."

"They must be worth a fortune!" George gasped.

Sally nodded. "They would be, except that to this day their whereabouts are a mystery."

"This house is full of mysteries," Bess remarked.

Nancy sat lost in thought. Then she asked, "Who first saw the ghosts, and when did the haunting begin?"

"Trass Sabuch," Sally responded. "The night he buried the dogs. At exactly nine o'clock, the hour when the dogs usually came in for the night, he heard whimpering. Puzzled, he looked toward the graves. There, among the trees, he saw four pairs of yellow eyes. Suddenly the creatures rushed at him. The howling and snarling were horrible. He rushed back inside and shut the door. In a flash, the house seemed surrounded. They clawed and scratched, throwing themselves against the doors and windows. The noise was terrifying. Finally the dogs retreated to the hilltop. There, over the graves of their dead masters, they howled mournfully until dawn." She drew a breath. "Trass never saw their bodies and in the morning he could find no tracks, but the house was covered with claw marks. That day he moved to a cabin on the far side of the lake and never set foot on the McDonald property again after dark."

Chills ran down the girls' spines.

"Trass Sabuch told us that it was the dogs' mistaken burial that had caused the haunting."

"And your family believed him?" Nancy asked.

Sally shook her head. "My grandfather was skeptical. He tried to stay one night, but had exactly the same experience."

Suddenly the front door crashed open. Wind

swirled through the room. The dying fire roared to life. Sally screamed. Bess gasped and clung to her startled cousin.

Nancy dashed to the door and bolted it securely. Darkness had fallen. The young detective glanced at the time. Five minutes to nine! The others, too, had noticed the approach of the haunting hour.

"Let's play a word game," Nancy proposed abruptly. Bess and George stared at her in disbelief.

George sniffed. "Nancy Drew, you have had some crazy ideas, but—"

"It'll be fun," she interrupted, "and distracting," she added, nodding toward Sally. Her chums looked. Sally was staring anxiously out the dark windows.

The game began, moving slowly at first, but picking up as everyone started to relax.

"Famous names beginning with William or Bill," Nancy proposed. "William Shakespeare," she offered.

"My favorite author," Sally joined in.

Nancy was relieved. "I would have loved to live at the turn of the sixteenth century when his plays, like *Hamlet*, were first performed," Sally continued.

"William McKinley," said George next. "Twenty-fifth president of the United States."

Bess thought for a moment. Finally she said, "William Dunbar."

"Who's he?" George challenged skeptically.

"The best football player at Dave's school," was the retort.

Nancy and George snickered. Sally was told that

Dave Evans was Bess's special friend. Soon everyone was laughing, including the mischievous Bess.

Suddenly Sally sat bolt upright. The color drained from her face. The others stared at her.

"Hear them?" she asked.

In a moment, the spine-chilling sounds reached their ears. Somewhere off to the side of the house agonized whimpering echoed through the trees.

"The ghosts!" Sally hissed.

The pitiful crying suddenly erupted into savage barking and growling. Chills again ran down the girls' spines. Nancy leaped to the window. The others seemed frozen. She gazed toward the ice house. Her breath stopped. There, among the dark trees, four pairs of glowing yellow eyes stared back at her!

"The ghost dogs!" George gasped.

By now Nancy's companions had ventured up behind her. Sally trembled violently as the girls huddled together. They watched in strange fascination while the eyes circled around. The black of the night was a flawless background. The pale moon could cast no light on the creatures. The eyes seemed to float without form. All at once, the ghosts advanced. The horrible sounds grew louder and louder.

"Oh!" Bess shrieked. She fled to the nearest corner and covered her eyes.

The others seemed transfixed. Suddenly the eyes vanished. The noises stopped. An eerie silence enveloped them. The girls inched forward. They craned their necks and peered out into the darkness.

Just then something huge and inky-black banged

against the glass. Snarling and barking, the creature clawed wildly at the window. Sally screamed. The four girls staggered backward as the window shuddered violently.

The dogs had surrounded the house! Eyes appeared at every window. Spine-chilling scratching and clawing sounds filled the air. The barking and snarling grew to an unbearable pitch. Terrified, the girls backed into the center of the room. Yellow eyes stabbed the darkness. There was another crash. The front door buckled. Then the handle rattled furiously. Bess wailed.

An eternity seemed to pass. Suddenly the sounds faded. The attack stopped. The dogs were moving away! Bess lifted her head. She opened her mouth, but Nancy raised her hand for silence.

They listened. The four ghostly animals could now be heard up on the hill. There, as the story foretold, they began to howl mournfully.

The ordeal had been exhausting. Nancy gently placed Sally on the sofa. Bess and George collapsed into chairs.

There must be an answer to this haunting, Nancy mused. I intend to find it, she resolved suddenly and started for the door.

"Nancy!" Sally cried. "Don't you dare go out there."

Her friend was becoming hysterical, so Nancy quickly reassured her. "I'll wait. I'll wait," she promised soothingly. Bess and George also seemed relieved.

"Let's get some sleep," Nancy suggested.

"If we can," Bess said shakily. The distant howling continued.

Nancy was glad that her friends fell asleep the moment they tumbled into bed.

The young detective, however, was restless. I wanted to get a closer look at those ghosts, she thought impatiently.

Nancy puzzled over the girls' ordeal until dawn. Suddenly, she realized the howling had ceased. Not waking the others, she stole out into the cool morning.

Fog swirled among the trees. Persistent wind whipped the branches. Nancy was suddenly startled by whispering voices.

"Who's there?" she demanded. Sheepishly, she realized it was the wind in the trees.

She laughed. "No wonder it's called Whispering Oaks," she said in relief.

The amateur sleuth examined the house. It was covered with deep claw marks. Below them were old, weathered grooves.

The dogs have been here before, she concluded, just as Sally had said.

Nancy scanned the ground. There were no tracks. So far, the evidence confirmed the old family story. Suddenly, something on the ground caught her sharp eyes. She kicked aside fallen leaves.

The soil has been overturned, she realized excitedly, and the disturbed earth forms a sort of path to the ice house.

Nancy followed the marks. Soon she found herself faced by a chilling sight. Behind the ice house, in the pale light, four inscribed gravestones stood side by side.

Nancy read the names aloud: KOSOB, SHROSE, DRAGENS, and NESCAIN. Puzzled, she memorized the dogs' strange names. I must ask Sally about them, she resolved.

Again, Nancy contemplated the pathway. There was a flaw in the story. They're not tracks, she mused, but these ghosts do disturb the ground as they move. Suddenly, her thoughts were interrupted. Through the trees she was startled to see two men talking. Nancy ducked into nearby foliage.

Stealthily she crept forward. When she got as close as she dared, their voices reached her.

"You'd better buy plenty of them," the older man said in a stern tone. "We don't need trouble with those girls here."

Nancy did not like the way the tall, powerful man said, "those girls." He had graying red hair and a cruel-looking mouth. His dark eyes shifted nervously.

His younger companion looked worried. He stifled a yawn. This angered the other.

"Now get going," he growled, "and don't you dare miss him."

The younger man was dark and, although smaller, seemed equally powerful. His face was kinder, but Nancy was sure the two men were related.

Who are they? she wondered shifting her position.

39

Just then a loud crack resounded through the woods—Nancy had stepped on a fallen branch.

The two men started, then disappeared. Nancy burst from her hiding place to follow, but they had vanished. She walked pensively back to the graves. I wonder who the "him" is they're afraid of missing?

Nancy decided to return to the house. Again, she passed the strange igloo-shaped ice house. Curious, she ventured to the opening and peered down into the cool darkness. Suddenly, she was pushed roughly from behind. With a cry, the young sleuth disappeared down into the dark hole.

Meanwhile, inside the house, Nancy's absence began to alarm her companions. "Where can she be?" Sally wailed. "What if she went outside before daylight!"

"Nancy wouldn't break her promise without a good reason," declared George quickly.

"I never should have brought us to this place," Sally berated herself.

"I think we ought to start looking for Nancy," Bess insisted. The ordeal of the previous night was still fresh in her mind.

George agreed. "It was broad daylight when someone tried to push that tree onto us. Nancy could be in real trouble."

The girls nervously began a search of the grounds. The dull morning and chilling winds made them shiver.

Apprehensive, they walked up the hill. The top was bare except for a large headstone. They proceeded along the lake.

"Look! Footprints!" George cried suddenly. "They're Nancy's sneakers!"

The three girls separated, calling her name loudly.

". . . the ice house," came a distant reply.

They ran to the structure. "Nancy?" Bess called through the opening.

"Get me out of here," she begged from below. "It's creepy."

Relieved, Sally and Bess ran for a rope and flashlight.

"What happened?" George called down as they waited. Nancy told her all about what had happened. "Do you think those men pushed you?" George asked, frowning.

Before Nancy could answer, Sally and Bess returned, breathless. Nancy hugged the wall so the flashlight could be thrown down safely.

Quickly she explored her icy prison. The round ice house was made of stone and extended deep into the cold ground. Leaves covered its floor. Fortunately, they had cushioned Nancy's fall.

She pushed some aside. To her surprise most of the stone slabs had been removed from the floor and deep holes had been dug into the ground. She looked at the walls. There, too, stones were missing, revealing similar holes.

Finally a rope snaked down to her, and she was pulled to the top. "I thought you'd never find me,"

Nancy gasped as she reached her friends.

"Not another word," George commanded. Shivering, Nancy was led back to the house and a roaring fire in the fireplace. Only after some breakfast did they allow the girl detective to tell her story. She ended by thanking her rescuers.

"You could have been seriously injured," Sally said with concern.

"It was probably that 'tree chopper,' " George remarked, "or those strange men you saw."

"But those men are Trass Sabuch's sons," Sally protested. "My family trusts them completely." She apologized for not warning the girls that the men still lived nearby. "The older man, Red, worked here with Trass as a boy. Jimmy, the younger one, joined Red after Trass's death. They keep an eye on the farm now."

Nancy listened thoughtfully. The dogs were apparently spectres, but whoever was trying to harm the girls was very real. They would have to live close by. Red and Jimmy were obvious suspects. But why would they not want us here? Nancy reflected.

As the girls exchanged guesses about the incident, Sally was quiet. Suddenly, she said, "It's too dangerous here. Ghosts haunt us at night and now someone tries to harm us during the day. I think we should leave. We'll walk down to the store and intercept my husband. Once we're there, we can phone Red and Jimmy. With their help Jeff could move the tree so we'd be able to come back for your car, Nancy. Then, we'll leave this farm to its ghosts—forever!" Her eyes brimmed with disappointed tears. The others were stunned.

"Sally, we want to stay," Nancy assured her. The others nodded. "We'll make a bargain," she urged. "If we can't solve the mystery before Jeff arrives, we'll go back."

Sally hesitated a few seconds, then gave each one a grateful hug and agreed.

"I'd like to solve the mystery surrounding this place," Nancy quickly said. "Tell me, why are those holes in the floor and walls of the ice house?" Her friends could offer no explanation.

"We could ask Red or Jimmy if we see them," Sally suggested.

"We'd better get him to move the tree for Jeff in any case," Nancy added as she scribbled on some paper. "What do you think of our ghosts' names?" They stared at the four words in puzzled silence.

"We were instructed to put the dogs' correct names on the stones," Sally said. "They were always called by nicknames. My grandfather eventually found the real names on their pedigree papers."

"They sound like Indian deities," Bess remarked, "not names for pet dogs." All the girls agreed the names were unusual.

"Did the will leave instructions for their own epitaphs?" George asked.

"Yes, but I don't remember the inscriptions," Sally answered.

"Let's go see them," Nancy urged.

The four girls soon reached the hilltop gravestones.

Below the conventional inscriptions were the enigmatic words:

> "Whosoever loves us shall hold us forever through the pages of time."

"That's weird," Bess commented.

"I wonder if it's a clue," Nancy said as she started down the hill.

George, an experienced camper, suddenly exclaimed, "Someone has been digging around here!"

Nancy was startled. "Why do you think that?"

"Because everywhere there are signs of quickly covered holes."

Nancy examined the ground where George was pointing. "You're right, George. It does look as if someone has been looking for something around here."

"But what?" Sally demanded.

"Another mystery," Nancy replied, staring into space. "Maybe whatever it is has some connection with that episode in the ice house."

The girls finally returned to the house. They shuddered as Nancy pointed to the splintered claw marks. She also related her discovery of the pathway of disturbed soil.

Sally sighed. "This detective work only seems to uncover more mystery."

"That's it." George grinned. "We find the clues, then Nancy figures it all out."

The young detective seemed not to hear her. She was deep in thought.

"Tell us more about the missing gold statues," Bess begged Sally as they ate lunch.

"Well, my grandfather thought that they were still somewhere at Whispering Oaks. That's really why he went to the farm that night. He was worried, though, and none of us has looked for them since."

All at once Nancy had an inspiration. "What did the McDonalds enjoy most in their lives?" she abruptly asked Sally.

Sally thought for a moment. "Probably their family, then Whispering Oaks, their dogs, horses, the garden, and reading." To prove this, she led the girls to the library. Every foot of wall space was covered with shelves of books. Each shelf was labeled.

"Canines, Horses, Gardens," Bess read.

"What are you up to?" George asked Nancy. The young detective wore a knowing smile and her eyes twinkled.

"I have a hunch the golden statues are hidden right here in this farmhouse," she announced.

Settled before a crackling fire, Nancy revealed her theory. "The McDonalds hid the valuable statues at Whispering Oaks after they were made. They wanted only your family to have them, Sally, so in the will they placed instructions concerning where to find them."

"So where are they?" asked George impatiently as the others nodded.

"The key is the answer to the riddle of the gravestones," Nancy said mysteriously. " 'Whosoever loves us shall hold us forever through the pages of time,' " she recited. "But we still have to figure out the dogs' mysterious names before we find the key to *where* the statues are hidden."

Suddenly there was a heavy thud against the house. Nancy bounded to the window and threw it open. Dry leaves rushed through the casement. Warding them off with her hand, she peered outside. Nothing!

I wonder if someone was listening outside the window, Nancy thought. Red or Jimmy? And if so, why?

Nancy returned and put the dogs' names in front of the girls. Bess grabbed a dictionary. For a while, they studied the strange words.

"Those ghosts could tell us the answer," George remarked with a grin.

"Maybe they're trying to!" Nancy cried to the others' astonishment. "What if Trass was wrong and the dogs haunt the farm because their statues have not been recovered by the McDonalds? They try to enter the house to tell us that the statues are inside."

Sally seemed struck by what her friend had said.

"I have a plan," Nancy continued. "I want to watch the ghosts tonight."

"Nancy, please don't take any risks," Sally implored. She was still convinced that the ghosts were evil.

"Jeff will be here by then," Bess reminded her. "He'll help us."

"George and I will slip outside before nine and hide," Nancy planned, "where we can watch as the ghosts move toward the house. I'm sure it will give us some answers."

"Thanks for volunteering me," George said with a smirk.

Sally jumped as a loud knock sounded at the door. Expecting Jeff, she ran to it. Red Sabuch loomed into the room. He spoke to her, then left hurriedly.

"Jeff is going to be late," Sally announced with dismay. "Jimmy has just returned from the store. Jeff is there, but his car has broken down. When Jimmy left him an hour ago, Jeff told him he would try to arrive here before dark."

"I'm sure he'll make it," Nancy said encouragingly.

"Did you ask Red about all the digging?" George asked, pursuing Nancy's discovery.

Sally answered distractedly. "He knows nothing about it . . . told me girls who stay in haunted houses often imagine things or exaggerate them . . . and promised to help move the tree."

George was incensed. "Imagine—exaggerate! I think those holes mean that Nancy isn't the first one to think the missing statues are here." The others agreed.

Nancy thought of the stranded Jeff. She had hoped he would be here to help with her daring plan.

"Let's find hiding places while it's still light," she suggested. "I'll watch the gravesite. George, suppose you keep an eye on the house."

The two girls went outside while the others prepared dinner. Eventually Nancy and George found suitable hiding places.

"Nancy, look over there!" George whispered suddenly. The Sabuch brothers were watching them intently. When they saw the girls staring back, they hurried away toward their cabin. Nancy and George exchanged suspicious glances and went back inside.

Over dinner the four girls discussed the plan. They agreed to use flashlights for signaling: two flashes, all clear; the light left on, trouble.

Two hours passed. A pitch-black night descended. Jeff had not arrived. Sally paced the floor.

"We'd better hide," Nancy finally announced. "It's already twenty minutes to nine."

As Sally wrung her hands, Nancy tried to reassure her. "Jeff should be here any minute."

Their companions remained visible in the house while Nancy and George crept silently out the side door, which they left unlocked in case they had to return in a hurry. Soon, they settled in their hiding places.

No moon, Nancy thought. A perfect night for ghost watching.

However, she could barely distinguish the four gravestones from her position.

For what seemed hours, the girls waited. Suddenly, Nancy caught her breath. Four pairs of yellow eyes materialized over the graves. Her spine tingled.

Despite the horrible whimpering of the dogs, Nancy edged forward. She had to see these canine ghosts. Their eyes began roving round and round. A cacophony of chilling sounds now surrounded Nancy. She inched closer and closer, her own eyes glued to the creatures. Unfortunately, one foot caught on a fallen branch. With a muffled cry, she fell heavily to the ground.

The sounds stopped. The four pairs of eyes turned in Nancy's direction. She dared not even breathe. Motionless, the creatures scanned the trees where she lay. Suddenly they moved directly toward her!

Nancy scrambled to her feet. The horrible sounds again resounded through the woods. A cold fear gripped her. Two pairs of eyes vanished. Nancy whirled around. Snarling, the two creatures now stood directly behind her!

In desperation Nancy bravely raised her flashlight, prepared to fight off the animals. Something abruptly caused her to lower the weapon. One of the approaching eyes flickered. Then it disappeared. Only three eyes glared at her. Nancy pointed her flashlight. Summoning courage, she turned the powerful beam directly on the mysterious creature. What she saw made her gasp. But at that instant a heavy blow hit her from behind. Nancy crumpled to the ground, unconscious!

Sally and Bess watched frantically from the window. They knew something was terribly wrong. The dogs had suddenly disappeared. Through the trees only the steady beam of a flashlight pierced the darkness.

"What shall we do?" Bess wailed helplessly.

Sally was as white as a sheet. Both girls seemed immobile.

Presently, soft scratching sounds broke the eerie silence. The girls were seized with terror. With a groan, the front door slowly began to open. Sally screamed. Bess panicked and threw her flashlight against the door. There was a crash as it shattered against the wood.

"Hey! What's going on?" a surprised male voice cried out.

"Jeff!" Sally exclaimed as he hesitantly entered.

She ran to her husband and collapsed in his arms. Color rushed to Bess's face as she sputtered an apology.

"Now calm down," the tall, attractive man said gently, "and tell me what happened."

The girls hurriedly briefed him. Jeff's face showed deep concern. From the moment Sally voiced her plan to visit Whispering Oaks, he had scoffed at the ghostly danger. Now he was sure that Nancy and George were in serious trouble.

"You stay here," he commanded. "I'm going to look around." He took Sally's flashlight. "Now I'm *really* sorry I didn't get here this morning."

Sally and Bess looked puzzled.

"Didn't Red give you my phone message that I'd arrive at noon instead of six?" Jeff asked.

Sally frowned. "He told us around six that when Jimmy left the store at five o'clock, you—"

"Five!" Jeff exclaimed. "I met a man who told me he was Jimmy Sabuch at eleven-thirty this morning. I stopped to buy something. When I came out, he was standing there with packets of batteries in his hands. My car wouldn't start, so he offered to take a message back to you."

"Why did Jimmy go down to the store this morning and wait until six to tell us you were there?" Bess questioned.

Jeff frowned. "I don't know. What I do know is that it took all day to repair a mysterious hole in my gas tank. At the time, I thought a malicious prankster had done it. Then, I finally arrive, and someone has chopped a tree down over the road. I had to walk the rest of the way!"

"But Sally told Red to move that tree hours ago!" Bess said in a strained voice. "And we already had bought plenty of batteries at the store."

Jeff was furious. The conclusion was obvious.

"But why would Red and Jimmy want to prevent you from reaching us?" Sally asked anxiously.

"I intend to find out," he declared angrily, "then call the police. Nancy and George's disappearance may not be so mysterious." Following Sally's directions, he stormed off toward the Sabuch cabin.

Nancy's eyes fluttered open. She blinked to confirm that she was in total darkness. Her head reeled as she tried to use all her senses. The young detective was bound and gagged, propped against a wall on a hard floor. She could smell mothballs. Restricted hand movements told her that the walls and floor were wooden.

I'm probably in a clothes closet, she reasoned, still groggy. Suddenly to her left she caught the scent of George's shampoo.

George! Nancy remembered at once. Her head cleared as she wriggled toward her friend. Abruptly, she collided with George's inert form. Nancy placed an ear to her body. She was still breathing.

I must get us out of here, Nancy thought frantically. George could be seriously hurt!

Suddenly, angry voices reached her ears. She moved with difficulty to what was apparently the door. Red and Jimmy Sabuch were outside! They were arguing.

"I'll never give it up!" Red shouted.

"But she *saw* me!" Jimmy returned angrily.

Nancy could now clearly recall what her light had revealed. The ghostly creature before her had been a man, his body completely covered in black material. On each hand was a black glove with two yellow eyes attached.

"That girl has ruined everything!" Red shouted back. "They'll *all* pay for her snooping," he snarled.

"Don't hurt them!" Jimmy cried out. "Dad would never have approved of this. He only scared people so he could look for the gold statues. You're going too far. If you hurt them," he warned, "I'll—"

"You'll what?" Red taunted. "Leave?" Then he added, "Okay, brother, we'll *both* leave, but with those statues!"

"What are you going to do?" Jimmy asked worriedly.

Red gave a cruel laugh. "I hate to admit it, but that pesky detective is getting pretty close to where the gold is. We'll find it first though . . . you wait! Now put our things in the old trunk," he shouted, "and light that fire. We'll burn everything, including that Drew girl!"

Fire! Nancy thought desperately. Her heart was pounding.

She strained at her bonds. To her amazement, they fell away easily! With no time to wonder why, she removed the gag and groped for George. Her ropes, too, were only loosely secured. Nancy was bewildered. In a flash, she had broken open the flimsy closet door. She rushed to the small fire the Sabuch brothers had started and quickly extinguished it with a bed pillow. She snapped on a nearby lamp. A gasp escaped her lips. Smoke emanated from a smoldering rag in a large ashtray.

Jimmy? Nancy wondered. She touched, smelled, and then tasted the clear liquid sprinkled over the furniture. He used water instead of kerosene, she realized with relief. He never even tried to burn us.

At that instant, a tall sandy-haired man burst into the cabin. "Nancy Drew?" he panted.

"Jeff Butler?" she returned.

"Am I glad to see you!" he cried.

Nancy did not waste words as she and Jeff exchanged stories. In a moment, Jeff was on the phone to the police. Nancy gave George first-aid as she lay on the couch. After Nancy was assured that the other girl was all right, the three anxiously hurried back to the farm.

Dawn broke as Whispering Oaks came into view. Nancy dashed ahead. The house seemed strangely quiet. Suddenly the Sabuch brothers staggered out of the front door. Red wielded an ax in one hand, and a book in the other.

"I won't let you do it!" Jimmy hollered as the men struggled.

Suddenly Red saw Nancy and the others. Realizing he was trapped, he gave his brother a hard shove, dashed to his truck, and sped away.

"He won't get far," Nancy said as they reached Jimmy, a police siren wailing in the distance.

"I know," Jimmy mumbled. "I never moved the tree."

Nancy smiled at Jimmy as they helped him into the house. Sally and Bess rushed forward. They had been cowering in a corner, terrified. There was a confusion of voices. Finally, Nancy managed to settle everyone into chairs. The complete story was revealed.

"So all along, the Sabuch family were pretending to be ghosts to scare us away!" Sally exclaimed.

"That's right," Nancy said. "They needed a way to look for the statues. I don't think Jimmy wanted any more to do with it, though." She glanced at him. He seemed exhausted.

At that moment a police car pulled up. Two officers escorted Red Sabuch into the house. His face was livid.

"We apprehended him down the road, trying to move a tree," one officer explained.

"I told you to move that thing!" Red screamed at his brother.

"Jimmy didn't want you to get away," Nancy defended him.

Red's face became almost purple with rage. He lunged at Nancy, but the officers restrained him.

"I'll tell you everything," Jimmy suddenly declared. "My father knew that the McDonalds had hidden the golden statues on the farm. When they died, Trass became obsessed with the idea of having the gold, but he needed a safe way of searching for it. Then, Red invented the story about the mistaken burial. He was always clever! Our father buried the dogs up on the hill as the McDonalds wished. But Red told him to tell the family that by mistake he had buried the dogs behind the ice house. Then, the two of them moved away from the farm and circulated the story about the ghost dogs. Red thought of the idea of the battery-powered gloves with eyes. He was also good at imitating animal sounds. Later, after I joined him, we played tapes from hidden speakers in the trees."

"What about the claw marks?" Nancy asked.

"Those were made with a little steel rake placed in the gloves. Red was scared when you arrived," he continued. "He tried to stop you with that tree. He also sent me down to the store to stop Jeff and buy fresh batteries. We used to listen at windows. Red was really worried because he could see that Nancy was too smart, so he pushed her down into the ice house to hurt her. That was when I decided I had had enough. I didn't move the tree and I never replaced the batteries in the gloves."

"You also helped us escape from your cabin," Nancy added, relating the incident to the police.

"You idiot!" Red shouted.

The police led both men away, after explaining that because of Jimmy's conduct, they were sure the judge would deal lightly with him.

Alone again, Sally beamed at Nancy. "Now we can finally live in this grand old place!" she cried.

"It's a shame the statues were never found," George remarked sadly.

Nancy's eyes twinkled again. "I think I know where they are," she said, smiling. "And I think Red, with my help, was very close to finding them—judging from what was in his hand."

The others stared at her. The young detective wrote the letters of the dogs' names on four separate pieces of paper and handed them around.

"Rearrange the letters," she instructed, "and see what common words you can come up with."

In a moment, KOSOB, NESCAIN, DRAGENS, and SHROSE became BOOKS, CANINES, GARDENS, and HORSES.

"Where have we seen books marked canines, gardens . . ."

"In the library!" Sally cried excitedly. "The statues must be behind those labeled shelves. Nancy, you're a genius!"

The young people hurried to the library. When the

three shelves marked canines, gardens, and horses were removed, a small door was revealed. Nancy pushed and prodded. Suddenly she found the spring. With a click, the door swung open. In an alcove were the exquisite gold statues of the four dogs!

The amazed onlookers carried the heavy treasure to the living room. Sally was teary-eyed. She threw her arms around Nancy.

"Thank you," she whispered. "Thanks to *all* of you."

"I don't know what to say," Jeff added emotionally.

"Just tell us that we can visit the farm again soon," Nancy said with a grin. "It would be lovely to return and hear *only* the whispering oaks . . . not howling dogs!"

Blackbeard's Skull

"**G**ood morning," Nancy Drew called out cheerfully as the park ranger walked up the sandy path. Nancy and her two girlfriends, Bess and George, had rented a cottage on the harbor of a small island off North Carolina.

"I hope you're ready for your private viewing of pirate gold, Nancy," pleasant, middle-aged Ranger Lane said with a chuckle. "Most people vacationing here on Pelican Island don't get out of bed this early."

"I'm wide awake and eager to see the doubloons!" Nancy assured him.

As they walked around the harbor to the ranger station, Lane told the attractive titian-haired eighteen-year-old that a local clammer had dredged up the doubloons off the northern coast of the island.

"Pelican," the ranger explained, "was a pirate hide-out as were other islands in the area. Blackbeard was killed not far from here in 1718. The Governor of

Virginia financed a ship with his own money and sent it down here with the sole purpose of putting an end to the pirate."

"It must have taken a clever and brave man to kill Blackbeard," Nancy commented.

"He had help," Ranger Lane replied. "Lieutenant Robert Maynard needed five bullets and twenty stabs of his sword to kill Blackbeard. Maynard cut off Blackbeard's head and stuck it on the bow of his ship. Or so the story goes. You should hear old George Habab sing the song he made up about Blackbeard's death."

"Could the doubloons on exhibit have belonged to Blackbeard?" Nancy asked.

"It's possible," Ranger Lane answered. "If so, I'd better watch out," he added with a wink. "Blackbeard left a deadly curse for anybody who stole his loot." The ranger slowed down his walk. "Here's the station."

The ranger station lay by the island's main docks. A flat, wooden building, it looked like a small warehouse with no windows and only one large door.

"The Coast Guard built this during World War II to house naval equipment," Ranger Lane explained in response to Nancy's puzzled expression. "Someday we hope to put up a real station."

Ranger Lane unlocked the heavy, wooden door and pushed it open.

"Here's the old chest," he began to say, then gasped.

Nancy followed his blank stare. A skull rested on an old piece of ship's bow in an otherwise empty corner.

"The doubloons! They're gone!" the ranger exclaimed. He glared at the skull, then whispered,
"Blackbeard!" The ranger began to look around. "I
don't see how anyone could have gotten in."

"When did you last see the gold?" Nancy asked.

"Yesterday evening," the ranger replied. "I checked
it before I locked up for the night. Maybe this is part of
the curse!"

"Did anyone else have access to the room after you
left?" Nancy gently questioned the agitated man.

"No, I have the only key," Ranger Lane answered.
"Wait," he added suddenly. "My assistant, Arthur
Huber, ran back in for a minute to get his glasses, but
he didn't carry anything out. There was a strong clear
plexiglas cover bolted to the chest to safeguard the
coins. Besides, I trust Arthur," Ranger Lane concluded firmly.

"Are you sure the door was locked behind him?"
Nancy asked.

"I double-checked it myself," the ranger declared,
"and it was locked this morning."

Nancy glanced around the station. Nothing except
the gold seemed to have been disturbed.

"I'm afraid headquarters won't be too pleased with
this," Ranger Lane sighed.

"I'm sure you protected the gold as well as anyone
could have," Nancy comforted the ranger.

She examined the station while Ranger Lane went
to alert the Coast Guard and sheriff. She found no
clues near the skull or elsewhere in the building, and
decided to have a look outside.

Nancy walked along the edge of the dock next to the station. Peering into the water below, she suddenly collided with an elderly man, teetered back and forth for a moment and almost tumbled off. Gaining back her balance quickly, she just managed to catch the old man before he fell.

"I'm so sorry for bumping into you," Nancy apologized breathlessly.

"I fear I was asleep at the helm myself," the man volunteered in a strong British accent. "No harm done, thanks to your excellent footwork."

Nancy introduced herself.

"I'm Colin Hudson," the white-haired gentleman responded. "I just arrived from England."

"What brought you to Pelican Island?" Nancy asked.

"I served off the island in a trawler during World War II," Mr. Hudson replied.

"Off this island," Nancy exclaimed. "I didn't realize the war got that close!"

"U-boats picked off a number of your merchant boats before we arrived to help," Mr. Hudson said. "Your navy wasn't used to fighting submarines."

"I would guess that's a pretty tricky business," Nancy ventured.

"Deadly tricky," Mr. Hudson agreed. "Indeed," he added sadly, "a U-boat sank my ship, the *Lancaster*. Some of my mates may lie in the graves at the British cemetery here."

"I noticed a British flag over one of the cemeteries and wondered why it was there," Nancy said.

62

"The people of Pelican very kindly donated a grave-yard for my countrymen who were killed at sea off the island during the war. I wanted to see that cemetery and visit the wreck of the *Lancaster*," the elderly man told Nancy.

"I'm sorry your ship was lost," Nancy said softly. "But I'd love to hear some of your stories of those times, and so I'm sure would my friends. Would you like to come to our cottage and have dinner with us tonight?" Nancy asked.

Mr. Hudson's face brightened. "I'd be delighted," he said, smiling.

"I have a special island recipe I'd like to try," Nancy continued. "If you don't mind, I'll test it out on you. Is seven o'clock a good time?"

"Perfect," Mr. Hudson replied.

Moments later, Ranger Lane returned, and Nancy quickly explained about the theft to Mr. Hudson. Then, politely excusing herself, she added, "See you at dinner." Swiftly she followed the somber-looking Ranger Lane into his office.

"I'm afraid I can't report any leads," he said in a low tone. "I just can't figure out how anybody got in the station. It almost makes me believe it was Black-beard's ghost. The Coast Guard is searching all the boats in the harbor. That's the best we can do for now."

"Maybe they'll find something," Nancy said sooth-ingly.

"I hope so, but I doubt it," the ranger replied. "I certainly appreciate your help, Nancy, whether we find the gold or not."

Nancy decided to take another look around the exhibit room. Kneeling on the rough-hewn wood floor, she scrutinized the skull. Peering at it from an angle, Nancy noticed an odd dark patch on one of the skull's back teeth. It had a filling in it!

Keeping this observation to herself, Nancy returned to her cottage.

Bess and George listened wide-eyed as she told them about her morning.

"I think our sleuth has found herself another mystery," boyish George teased Nancy.

Plump, pretty Bess shivered. "I don't like that skull being left there," she declared. "I hope Blackbeard's ghost doesn't try to get me!"

"Don't be so superstitious," George chided her cousin.

"I found a clue that should make you less worried about Blackbeard's ghost," Nancy said, her eyes twinkling. "The skull has a filling in one of its teeth."

"Couldn't Blackbeard have had cavities?" Bess interrupted.

"I'm sure he did," Nancy chuckled. "But I doubt he ever visited a dentist!"

"The whole thing must be a hoax," George frowned.

"I think you're right," Nancy agreed. "But we still haven't figured out how anyone but a ghost could have broken into the ranger station."

"Now that you have a mystery, Nancy, are we still

going to the beach this afternoon as we planned?" Bess teased her friend.

"You bet," Nancy replied smiling. "Pelican Island has a lovely beach and I don't want to miss having a swim."

The girls spent a pleasant day in the water and sunbathing.

"I'm going to need help gathering dinner," Nancy announced mysteriously when the afternoon was almost over. Bess and George looked puzzled.

"I'd like to make coquina chowder tonight," Nancy explained, "and we need a bucket of coquina clams."

"They're the shells that look like tiny butterflies!" Bess exclaimed.

The three friends dug for coquinas in the wet sand as the waves washed back and forth around them. Soon they had filled a bucket.

Afterward, George and Bess dropped Nancy off at the ranger station on the way back. Ranger Lane had no news. He introduced Nancy to a young, slightly built, spectacled man.

"Nancy, I'd like you to meet Arthur Huber, my assistant," Ranger Lane said. "Nancy here has been helping us try to solve the burglary," the ranger informed Huber.

"How did you become involved?" he asked her curtly.

"Nancy was with me when I discovered that the gold was gone," Ranger Lane interjected.

"I appreciate the young lady's curiosity," the assistant snapped. "But I think we can handle this problem ourselves."

Embarrassed by his subordinate's rudeness, Ranger Lane hastily escorted Nancy out of the station.

"Arthur's been very jumpy lately, especially today since the gold disappeared," he apologized. "Please excuse him."

Nancy felt that the young man's behavior had been uncalled for, but kept her thoughts to herself.

Somewhat ruffled by the encounter with Arthur Huber, Nancy was thoughtful as she walked back around the harbor to the cottage. Once she reached the cottage, however, she busied herself preparing the coquina chowder with her two friends.

Nancy, George, and Bess peeled potatoes and onions and threw them in with the boiling coquinas. The percolating soup smelled delicious, and the friends couldn't resist a taste.

"Mmmm," George commented as she gingerly sampled a hot spoonful. "I can see why the islanders like to eat this stuff."

Bess made some grilled tomato, cheese, and onion sandwiches to round out the dinner. She and George sat on the porch to wait for Mr. Hudson while Nancy changed out of her dungarees.

"I love the pink light on everything," Bess sighed as she watched the evening sky. "The sailboats look especially pretty."

"What a gorgeous sunset!" Nancy agreed, stepping onto the porch.

Mr. Hudson still had not arrived when the sun was completely gone.

"I wonder why he's late," Nancy remarked in a somewhat worried tone. "I think I'll go look for him."

"We'll stay here in case he shows up," George volunteered.

Nancy walked all the way around the harbor in the rapidly fading light but saw no sign of the Englishman. Realizing she was near the British cemetery, Nancy decided to look there for the elderly man.

The absence of street lamps made it difficult for Nancy to see, but she moved ahead slowly. Soon a dimly lighted lamp post and a British flag waving in the breeze appeared by the side of the road. Nancy picked her way to the small fenced-in plot. Mr. Hudson was not there, but Nancy caught sight of a plaque listing the British sailors who had died. Suddenly she started. One of the names was Colin Hudson!

Spooked, Nancy headed back along the dark road toward the harbor. As she reached it, the young sleuth heard a banjo being played and a voice singing. Nancy caught the words, "British boys." Following the sound, she came upon a weatherbeaten-looking old man sitting on the front porch of a store. He was the singer and banjo player.

"Hello," Nancy called out.

The old man jumped.

"You scairt the livin' daylights outta me," he growled.

"I'm sorry," Nancy apologized. "You must be

67

George Habab. Ranger Lane told me you compose your own songs."

"Ranger Lane considers me a historic landmark of sorts," he commented, pleased that Nancy had heard of him. "Made up that song I was just singing," he admitted. "I felt powerful sorry for those English boys who kept washin' up in '42."

Nancy asked Mr. Habab about her British friend, but the banjoist could not recall seeing him.

"Reckon dinner just slipped his mind," he said.

Nancy doubted that but thanked the islander and secured a promise that he would play her his Blackbeard song before she left for home.

Nancy hurried over to the Coast Guard station. A young man sat at the night desk. He could supply no information about Mr. Hudson. As Nancy walked out the door, however, the coast guardsman called her back.

"Have you talked to Gerald Curran?" he asked. "He's a World War II buff who's always scuba diving around wrecks. Curran owns that big catamaran moored in the harbor, but he spends nights in a cottage he rented."

Nancy thanked the young man and got directions to Curran's cottage, which was not far from her own. He also insisted that Nancy borrow his large flashlight.

"It gets awfully dark and a little scary here at night," he said. "You can bring the flashlight back tomorrow."

Guided by the powerful beam, Nancy hurried back to her cottage.

"Nancy, where were you?" Bess called out as her friend neared the cottage, "Did you find Mr. Hudson?"

"No," Nancy reported ruefully, "but I have one more lead to investigate."

"Mr. Hudson must have forgotten he was to eat dinner with us," George suggested. "Maybe he fell asleep."

"He seemed so excited about coming I can't believe he could have," Nancy replied, frowning. Secretly, she was beginning to think he had had an accident.

"I wish we knew where he was staying," kindhearted Bess sighed.

"Well, I might be able to find out," Nancy said hopefully. Quickly she told her two friends about Gerald Curran.

"If I don't learn anything from him, we can start to check hotels and cottages in the morning," she said.

George offered to accompany Nancy to the scuba diver's cottage, but Nancy, knowing that Bess would be afraid if left alone, insisted on going by herself.

Nancy strode toward the diver's cottage. The sandy lane was as dark as the coast guardsmen had warned her it would be. The flashlight she carried was the only light besides those in the cottages. Reaching what she thought was the right cottage, she walked up to it shining her flashlight in front of her. A light shone from the back porch.

"Hello. Anyone home?" Nancy called out.

"Who is that snooping around here?" an unfriendly male voice demanded.

Taken aback, Nancy identified herself and explained why she had come.

"I'm sorry," the voice apologized. "I thought you were some nosy kid or tourist. I'm Gerald Curran. I'll let you in. Just a minute."

Nancy heard metal objects being pushed around. Then Gerald Curran opened the screen door. He was a blond, heavy-set, muscular man. Nancy guessed that he was in his late thirties. Rusty pieces of naval equipment cluttered the porch. Nancy almost banged her shin on an old propeller blade.

"Sorry to bother you," Nancy said, "but I hoped you might have seen Mr. Hudson."

"No," the scuba diver replied, shaking his head. "I can't think of anyone like that."

"He might have been out at the *Lancaster*," Nancy remarked.

The skin diver seemed startled but quickly collected himself.

"I'm sure I would have seen him if he had been," he said firmly. "I pass the *Lancaster* every day. As a matter of fact I was near it most of the day today. Hudson couldn't have visited it ... Why are you looking for him?" Curran concluded.

"He's a friend," Nancy replied simply. "He was supposed to come over to dinner tonight at our cottage."

"Is he a close friend?" Curran asked sharply.

"Close enough that I keep an eye on him," Nancy announced curtly, annoyed by the man's manner.

"Well, I wouldn't worry about him," Curran advised smoothly. "Most people like to wander around on their own when they visit this island. He's probably asleep. Or maybe he saw all he wanted to and took the ferry back to the mainland."

"Maybe you're right," Nancy said, but was unconvinced. "How did you become interested in World War II?" she asked in a friendly way.

"Hobby," Curran answered. "Also, I'm an expert scuba diver and it seemed like a good way to combine both interests."

"I noticed your catamaran out in the harbor," Nancy continued. "It's a beauty. Does it have living quarters?"

"Yes," Curran replied, "but too cramped for my tastes. I prefer the conveniences of a cottage."

Nancy nodded. "I'm sure the cottage is more comfortable, but I'd love to see your boat sometime."

Curran seemed somewhat irritated.

"It's not very interesting," he muttered, "but perhaps I'll show it to you sometime when I'm not busy. Where are you staying?"

"In the Monroe cottage on the harbor," Nancy informed him.

"Are you here alone?" Curran asked her.

"No, with friends," Nancy replied. "But I could easily be diverted for a look at your catamaran or at a World War II wreck." The girl felt that Curran knew more than he was volunteering, and she wanted an opportunity to interrogate him further.

"If I find time, I'll come by," Curran said. "Now, if you'll excuse me, I have work to do."

"Thank you for your help," Nancy called as she walked out the screen door. Curran muttered something in reply.

That night Nancy had troubled dreams. She was glad to be out of bed at dawn and decided to take the motorboat they had rented with the cottage and visit the wreck of the *Lancaster*. She left a note for the sleeping Bess and George and quietly put her scuba-diving equipment in the boat in case she needed it. Navigating by a map of wrecks which Ranger Lane had given her, Nancy motored out to the *Lancaster*.

To her surprise, she found Gerald Curran already at the wreck despite the early hour. He wore scuba-diving equipment and seemed not at all pleased to see Nancy. After barely waving at her, he jumped into the water. Nancy decided to go after him.

She dropped the anchor, set up the ladder, and put on her scuba gear. She jumped in next to the anchor line and climbed down it to the *Lancaster*.

The wreck looked blurred and ghostly in the dark gray water. Nancy saw no sign of Curran. As Mr. Hudson had explained, the *Lancaster* was not a real ship, just a small, converted trawler. Nancy thought admiringly of the British sailors who chased U-boats in these makeshift warships. Swimming around the trawler, the girl sleuth discovered a large hole in the hull where the submarine torpedo must have hit. Cautiously, she eased her way in. Then suddenly, without warning, something sharp fell on her head. It was a headless skeleton!

Never losing her composure, Nancy surfaced along

the anchor line quickly and deliberately. Curran had not returned to his boat. Nancy was convinced that the unpleasant man had something to do with the skeleton. She wondered why he was so determined to scare her away.

Nancy swam to her ladder, took off her fins and climbed up. She lifted the heavy air tank off her shoulders, then motored back into the harbor. The boat slapped up and down on the choppy early morning waves.

Bess and George stood on the dock of the cottage.

"Nancy!" Bess greeted her friend with relief. "I was afraid you might have bumped into a ghost at the wreck."

"Actually, a ghost bumped into me," Nancy reported wryly. She told her friend about the skeleton.

Bess flopped down weakly in a chair on the dock, but George spoke up angrily. "That man Curran is no good," she declared. "I'll bet he was responsible for this 'ghost.'"

Nancy agreed. She sat down in a chair next to Bess and looked thoughtful for a moment. Suddenly she jumped to her feet.

"I think our detective has a hunch," George said knowingly.

Nancy smiled at her friend. "You're right, George, but before I follow it, I think we should ask for Mr. Hudson at the hotels and cottages."

"That will take a lot of asking," George commented. "This island is packed with places to stay."

"Let's get started," Nancy urged.

"Wait a minute," Bess interjected. "How about a little breakfast before we turn into ghosts ourselves?"

George and Nancy laughed and admitted they were ravenous. Bess scrambled eggs, baked delicious cornbread, and fried some bacon by the time Nancy had showered and changed out of her swimsuit.

"Smells heavenly," Nancy grinned when she entered the cozy kitchen.

After breakfast, Bess insisted upon washing the dishes despite the other girls' protests.

"I love the view of the harbor through the kitchen window," she declared. "It makes me enjoy doing the dishes."

"I'm eager to look for Mr. Hudson," Nancy conceded, "but I claim cleaning up after dinner tonight."

Nancy and George divided the hotels and cottages for their hunt.

"I'll take the ones on the other side of the harbor," Nancy suggested. "Maybe you can get a look at Gerald Curran without his recognizing you."

"I'd like to punch him in the nose," George announced stoutly. "Dropping skeletons on people! The nerve of him!"

The girls' thorough investigation took Nancy and George most of the day and netted nothing.

"Mr. Hudson seems to have vanished into thin air," George complained when they met back at the cottage late that afternoon.

Nancy remembered the list of names in the British

cemetery that had included that of the missing Mr. Colin Hudson, but she kept it to herself. Nancy certainly didn't believe in ghosts, and felt there was no point in alarming her friends.

Bess reported that Gerald Curran had dropped by the cottage during their absence.

"He said you had been curious about his catamaran and his diving, Nancy, but I thought he was the one who was curious. He kept asking me questions about where you were and what you were doing, but I just said I wasn't sure and that I didn't know when you would be back."

Nancy praised Bess for her careful answers and the plump blond beamed. Then Bess exclaimed, "My goodness, it's almost dinner time and you two haven't even had lunch."

"Your breakfast lasted me all day," Nancy teased her friend. Actually she had had little appetite because of her concern about Mr. Hudson.

Nancy offered to pick up some fresh fish from Mr. Habab's store.

"That's a marvelous idea," Bess agreed. "I leafed through a local cookbook while you were out sleuthing and found some great recipes."

The cottage was equipped with bikes as well as a motorboat. Nancy chose one with a large wire basket in front. She started along the road circling the harbor at a leisurely pace. Musing on the stolen gold and Mr. Hudson's mysterious disappearance, she occasionally turned her head and glanced at the boats rocking gently in the harbor.

Suddenly a truck swerved by Nancy and forced her into the soft sand off the side of the road. Struggling to keep her bike from falling, Nancy barely had a chance to glance at the vehicle moving away from her. She did notice, however, that the truck was the light green of the Park Service!

Furious, Nancy pedaled to Ranger Lane's house. He was seated in a rocking chair on his front porch. Upset when Nancy told him of the incident, he promised to find out who had been driving.

"I'm sure you will," Nancy mollified the agitated man. "Fortunately I wasn't harmed."

"I can't think of anyone in the service who behaves like that." The ranger shook his head. "First the theft and now this."

When the ranger mentioned the theft Nancy remembered something she had wanted to ask him.

"May I borrow the key to the ranger station tonight?" she asked. "I'd like to take another look around."

"Of course," Lane replied. "I'd be happy to come with you."

"Thank you very much, but I think it would be better if I went alone," Nancy said. "I'd like to keep this trip secret and that's easier with one person," she explained tactfully. "Could you do me another favor and not tell *anyone* that I have the key?"

"Not a word," the ranger promised, "but I must admit you're making me very curious. I suppose you'll be safe."

"I'll give you a detailed report in the morning when

I return the key," Nancy assured him. "I'd better hurry and buy the fish I promised to get for dinner." She took the key and rushed to Mr. Habab's store.

"I was just about to close," he announced as Nancy walked in. "Did you ever find your friend?"

Nancy informed him of her unsuccessful search.

"Well, don't worry, little lady, I'm sure he'll turn up," the warm-hearted storekeeper soothed her. "Now, can I interest you in some fresh bluefish?"

Nancy bought some of the fish, which he wrapped in newspaper. He refused to let her pay for it. "I'll make you do a little singing for me sometime in payment," he declared. Nancy decided to buy him a gift before leaving the island and loaded the fish into the basket on her bike.

"Hope you don't get followed home by a parade of cats," Mr. Habab quipped as she set out. "They love my fish."

After a delicious dinner prepared by Bess, Nancy pondered Mr. Hudson and the doubloons as she washed the dishes. The young detective decided to wait until the middle of the night before going to the ranger station.

"Are you sure you'll be all right, Nancy?" Bess asked anxiously before going to bed.

"I'll be fine," Nancy reassured her friend. "No one knows I'll be in the ranger station tonight."

George offered to accompany Nancy, but the young sleuth preferred to go alone, as she believed it would be less conspicuous.

When Nancy left the cottage a few hours later, a

thick layer of clouds covered the night sky. Without stars, the moon, or street lamps, the harbor was pitch black. Nancy chose not to shine her flashlight so as to avoid being noticed. She listened to the musical clanking of sailboat rigging as she stole around the harbor. None of the cottages had lights on. Everyone seemed to be asleep.

As she neared the ranger station, Nancy thought she heard footsteps behind her. She stopped and listened intently. A boat was rubbing gently against the dock, and Nancy decided that was what she must have heard. The ranger station looked black and spooky. She was glad there were no windows in the building so that no one could see her flashlight.

Nancy slipped the heavy iron key into the door and silently swung it open. After shutting the door behind her, the young sleuth shone her flashlight on the floor of the station. Squatting on the rough wood, she examined the area under the chest, but found nothing. Nancy inspected the entire floor with no more luck.

Then she went directly to Arthur Huber's desk. Peering intently at the boards beneath it, Nancy discovered a latch cleverly hidden in the wood. She pressed it and a trapdoor opened to reveal water below. Suddenly a spooky shadow seemed to dance before her. "Blackbeard," she murmured softly, trembling despite her disbelief.

Moments later, something hit Nancy on the head from behind and pushed her into the water!

About an hour later, she awoke to find herself

bound, gagged, and suffering from a terrible headache. The girl detective glanced around and guessed
she was in the cabin of a catamaran, probably Gerald
Curran's, no doubt!

On the bunk across from her lay Colin Hudson! He
smiled as best he could although his mouth, like hers,
was gagged. Nancy winked back, determined that
they both keep up their spirits. The elderly British
gentleman looked pale and Nancy wondered angrily
if Curran had bothered to give him any food.

Nancy felt the catamaran start to move. After a
while it began rocking up and down and she knew
they were out of the small waves in the protected
harbor. The large hatch was shut and the cabin was
stuffy and uncomfortable.

All I need now is to get seasick for the first time in
my life, Nancy thought ruefully.

The sound of two voices came through a small open
porthole, which was the only source of fresh air.
Nancy recognized the voices of Gerald Curran and
Arthur Huber.

"That blasted girl!" Huber hissed. "The old man
was bad enough. But then, after our months of plan-
ning, she has to butt in."

"Cut it out," Curran said harshly. "No one knows
she ever even went into the station, and they won't be
able to get in until they break down the door. Remember, the only key is down at the bottom of the harbor
where we dropped it."

"But her friends will raise the alarm and the whole

Coast Guard will be out looking for her," Huber argued.

"They won't know she's gone until morning," Curran replied. "By that time she and the old man will be on a tiny island miles away. You'll be at work in the morning as if nothing had happened. I'll have the gold hidden in my World War II junk. By the time they find the girl and the old guy—if they do find them—I'll have gone home on the ferry with my loot and you'll have left too if you know what's good for you."

"They'll search the country for me," Huber whined.

"Oh, shut up," Curran barked rudely. "You're in it up to your neck now. So let's see if you can help me."

The men were quiet for some time as the boat sailed on. Then again Nancy heard their voices.

"The dawn's coming up," Huber said anxiously.

Nancy heard the sound of the anchor being dropped.

"And we're at the wreck just as I planned," Curran snarled back. "I'll have the gold up here in about fifteen minutes and then we can dump the girl and the old man. I hope it's not too hard for you to guard a tied-up teenage girl and an old man while I'm gone," Curran called out sarcastically. Nancy heard a splash as Curran jumped into the water.

Huber muttered after him, "You brainless muscled monkey!" Nancy thought wryly that the slight ranger had probably waited until Curran was underwater and out of earshot before he insulted him.

Realizing she had no time to lose, Nancy looked around the cabin for some way to attract attention.

Back at the cottage, neither Bess nor George slept soundly. They met each other in the kitchen.

"Worried about our detective?" George asked her cousin.

"Yes," Bess admitted. "She's been gone for hours. I know she doesn't want anyone to know she's at the station, but I'm scared something's happened to her."

"I am too," George agreed. "Let's walk to the ranger station. If we don't find Nancy there, we'll tell the Coast Guard she's missing."

George found a flashlight in a drawer but the battery was dead.

"I'm afraid it's going to be pretty dark out there," she warned Bess.

"I'm so worried about Nancy I don't care if I run into every ghost on the island," Bess declared stoutly. "Let's throw on some clothes and march to the station."

The two cousins hurried as best they could in the total darkness. Once Bess heard a funny noise and clutched her cousin's arm.

"It's only a toad," George informed her.

Bess apologized, then declared, "Toads or no toads, I'll make it to the ranger station or bust."

When they reached the building, George knocked loudly and called Nancy's name. There was no answer. The cousins rushed over to the Coast Guard station.

"I hate to think what might have happened to Nancy," Bess murmured.

Bess and George encountered the same coast guardsman whom Nancy had questioned the night before about Colin Hudson. The young man started in surprise when they told him about Nancy.

"The night patrol is still out," he informed them. "I'll alert Captain Doyle about Nancy immediately. Those on land duty will start to search around the ranger station and harbor. People seem to be disappearing on Pelican all of a sudden," he said in a puzzled voice. Then he called the night patrol on the large radio next to him.

"Why don't you girls accompany the land patrol?" he suggested. "I'm sure they'd appreciate any help you could give them."

Craning her neck to see behind her, Nancy spied a boat horn. Wasting no time, the agile sleuth twisted her body until her hip pressed against the horn. While Mr. Hudson watched in amazement, she beeped out SOS. The horn blared so loudly it almost deafened her.

"What are you doing?" a furious Huber yelled at Nancy as he scrambled down into the cabin. "You'll be overboard with your hands and feet tied if you pull another stunt like that." The man stiffened as he heard a Coast Guard siren off in the distance. Cursing

Nancy, the ranger turned on the boat radio. He put it on a rock station playing very loud music.

"That'll drown your screams," he sneered at Nancy. Then Huber clambered back on deck to await the Coast Guard.

"Ahoy there!" a hearty voice called out in a few minutes. "I'm Captain Doyle of the Coast Guard. We picked up your SOS."

"Sorry, Captain," Huber said smoothly. "I just wanted to make sure the horn worked. I figured no one would hear it."

"Say, you're one of the rangers, aren't you?" Captain Doyle asked.

"Yes," Huber replied, "I guess I'm sort of a landlubber. I didn't realize I had sent out a message."

"What are you doing on Curran's catamaran?" the captain questioned him.

"Gerald Curran said he found some World War II artifacts which he would let us exhibit at the station. I came out to have a look at the site," Huber said.

"Have you seen any sign of a reddish-blond eighteen-year-old girl?" Captain Doyle asked.

"Sorry to say I haven't," Huber answered. "Is somebody missing?"

"We had a radio message to be on the lookout for a Nancy Drew," Captain Doyle explained.

Fearing that the Coast Guard boat would pull away momentarily, Nancy thought quickly. Huber had moved the horn out of her reach. Nancy calculated that if she maneuvered her body into a shoulder stand she could get one foot in front of the porthole.

Fortunately, a young sailor caught sight of Nancy's foot. He went over to the captain and whispered in his ear.

"Could you come on board for a minute and sign some routine papers, Ranger Huber?" the captain requested. "Regulations, regulations," he complained. "With all this paperwork, it's a miracle I ever get to the open sea."

Huber unsuspectingly boarded the Coast Guard boat. Two sailors took his arm as if to help him aboard but then held the ranger firmly in their grasp.

"What is the meaning of this?" Huber protested, writhing in the grip of the burly sailors.

"One of my men caught sight of some unusual cargo," Captain Doyle said sternly. "Unless you can convince me that teenage girls are World War II artifacts, I think you're going to be in a lot of trouble."

Huber went limp. "It's all Curran's fault," he whined piteously.

"You must be quite a contortionist," Captain Doyle complimented Nancy as he untied her.

"I've learned a few gymnastics tricks," Nancy explained modestly to the attractive, bearded captain.

"I'm glad you did," he replied, "or we might never have found you. There are countless tiny islands around here where Huber and Curran could have abandoned you."

"I'm quite delighted myself that Nancy came along," Mr. Hudson spoke up as he vigorously rubbed his hands and feet where the ropes had been. "I never thought an old sea dog like myself would get sick of being on a boat, but this is one boat I'm eager to quit for good."

"Did Curran give you anything to eat?" Nancy asked.

"No," Mr. Hudson answered. "I think he was afraid that if he undid the gag I would yell—and I would have, too."

"We haven't seen Curran," Captain Doyle informed them.

"He dived down to the wreck," Nancy said. "He's picking up the doubloons they stole from the ranger station."

"Curran and Huber stole the gold?" the captain gasped.

Nancy nodded. "Perhaps if I confront Huber he'll confess."

Captain Doyle approved Nancy's plan. They climbed out of the hatch. Unassisted, Nancy jumped off the catamaran onto the Coast Guard boat.

Huber sat, sour and sulky, between the two sailors. They were so much bigger than the ranger that he looked like a naughty child.

"Curran and Huber were partners," Nancy began. "Working nights, Curran cut a hole in the ranger station floor from the water below. Huber drove thin spikes through the floor under his desk so Curran would know where to cut. The ranger also covered up any marks and made the latch for the trapdoor."

"Why didn't we see Curran?" Captain Doyle asked.

"He submerged and surfaced in the middle of his

catamaran," Nancy explained. "After the trapdoor was finished," she continued, "Huber pretended he had left his glasses in the station so he could run back in. Then he dropped the chest of gold through the trapdoor and replaced it with the skull."

"Where did they get the skull?" Captain Doyle questioned Nancy.

"From the *Lancaster*," Nancy replied. "Curran dropped the headless skeleton on me when I went down there."

"The idiot!" Huber cried out angrily.

Nancy continued to ignore the ranger. "Curran picked up the gold as soon as it got dark and hid it in the wreck at dawn. When the Coast Guard searched his catamaran the next day they found nothing."

"That's when I entered the scene," Colin Hudson volunteered. "I ran into Curran that morning after I talked to you, Nancy. He overheard me telling of my interest in the *Lancaster* and offered to take me to her."

"You must have found the gold," Nancy commented.

"Yes, I did," the old sailor affirmed. "I know the insides of the *Lancaster* better than I know myself. After I found it, this chap Curran, who hadn't bargained on me ever finding his loot, gave me rather a nasty knock on the head and, I guess, hauled me back to his catamaran."

"We must have searched it already," Captain Doyle said.

"Curran tried to stop me from exploring the wreck by dropping the skeleton on my head when I went out there the following morning," Nancy added. "That gave me an idea about where the skull had come from. Then I thought of a trapdoor. I thought Blackbeard had come to get me for a moment there!"

"You ruined everything," Huber exploded.

"Curran should surface any minute now," Nancy warned Captain Doyle.

"We'll make sure to grab him when he does," the captain declared.

Caught red-handed after surfacing with the gold and seeing his partner in custody, Curran confessed his part in the theft and kidnapping.

"Caught by a girl," he muttered dejectedly.

That evening, Nancy, Bess, George, and Mr. Hudson enjoyed a tasty dinner prepared by the grateful Ranger Lane and his wife.

"If you'll take a walk with me, I have a surprise for you," the ranger announced when they finished, his eyes twinkling.

He led his guests to George Habab's store. The old fellow sat on the porch grinning, his banjo in his hands. Without saying a word, he began to play and sing. "Here's the ballad of Nancy Drew," he began. The song went on to describe Nancy's adventures on Pelican Island.

Captivated, she and her friends listened intently. When the islander finished, they clapped loudly.

"It's even better than my Blackbeard song," George Habab claimed.

"You promised to play that for me," Nancy reminded him. The banjoist began, and Bess's eyes widened as the song told the story of Blackbeard's bloody death.

Nancy smiled and nodded her thanks, then asked, "Would you mind playing your British sailor song for Mr. Hudson?"

"Where is Mr. Hudson?" George asked. Everyone looked around. The old man had disappeared. Nancy finally told her friends how she had found the British man's name on the list of deceased at the cemetery.

"Reckon he came back to help us out, to kind of return the favor for us building that British cemetery," George Habab whispered softly.

"Without him, no one would have thought to go to the *Lancaster*," Nancy commented.

Then she looked at Bess, whose face had turned pale. "That's okay," Bess assured her friend, "I guess I can handle nice ghosts."

The
Ghost
Jogger

One evening, Nancy and her close friends, Bess and George, joined the young people of River Heights who gathered in the park to jog. The three girls became separated, however.

Nancy found herself running beside a figure wearing a long white cape, with a hood that completely covered his face.

Weird jogging outfit, she thought.

A moment later, the figure stuck his hand out, holding in it a folded note. The young detective quickly grabbed it, and unfolded it as she ran. The ink was mysteriously faded. But after staring at it closely she read:

> NANCY, FIND THEM IN THE EMPTY BARN WITH
> THE FLAMING HORSE ON IT.
> —THE FAMILY GHOST

"Who are you?" she asked, turning abruptly.

The ghostly being had disappeared!

Nancy's pulse skipped a beat. What was this strange vision?

Nancy tried to find the hooded ghost, but he had vanished in the evening dusk. She ran up to passing joggers and asked if they had seen him. Most of them said no, but two pointed off among some trees.

Nancy ran to the wooded area, but failed to locate the mysterious figure. As she started back, her pulse skipped another beat. For a moment, she thought she saw a flash of white in between the trees, but when she arrived at the spot there was nothing there.

Anxiously, the girl detective hurried back to the joggers, joined them to the park entrance, then dashed outside. Minutes later she reached home and burst into the living room.

Hannah Gruen, the motherly housekeeper for Nancy and her father, was in the den watching a newscast on TV. She looked up quickly and gasped.

"Nancy, you're as white as a sheet. This jogging is too much for you. You'd better ease up a bit."

"Oh, Hannah, dear, I'm all right. I just had a little scare, that's all."

"A mugger?" Mrs. Gruen asked nervously.

"No. A ghost." Nancy told Mrs. Gruen about the incident.

"I wonder . . ." the housekeeper said, but did not go on.

"You wonder what?" Nancy prodded her.

"If a story on the news could tie in with your adventure."

"What was the newscast about?" Nancy asked.

"That two children, a brother and sister, aged eight and ten, are missing. It's not known if they ran away deliberately, wandered off and are lost, or were kidnapped. The police have no clues."

"How dreadful!" Nancy replied, then perked up. "And you think, Hannah, that the ghost jogger may know something about it?"

Mrs. Gruen smiled. "I'll go a step further. I think he wants you to solve the mystery!"

"Why, Hannah, you're becoming a regular armchair investigator," Nancy commented with a grin. "I wonder if you could possibly be right," she added, turning her attention to the newscast and hoping the segment about the children would be repeated. It was not. She turned the dial on the set to several other channels but learned nothing more about the case.

Nancy turned off the television and sat lost in thought. What should she do? Work on the clue the ghost had given her, or wait until she saw him again? A few minutes later, Nancy picked up the phone and called George. "No, I'm all right," Nancy spoke from her end of the line, "but I had a terrible scare in the park after we were separated. Can you go with me tomorrow morning to chase down a clue or two?"

"Sure. A new mystery?"

"I think so. Okay. I'll pick you up at ten. Is Bess free?"

"No. I think she has plans tomorrow."

As soon as George was in Nancy's car the next day, she asked for a full explanation of where they were going and why.

"We have to find a deserted barn with a flaming red horse on it."

"Sounds rather hard to find," George commented. "What's the story?"

"I'm not sure, but *possibly* those two missing children are being held there."

"Wow!" George exclaimed. "And you expect me to help you rescue them?"

"You guessed it."

"I'll take a raincheck," said George with a joking smile. "If this *is* a kidnapping case, what's the ransom?"

For an answer Nancy told her friend about the ghostly being that passed a note to her. "Then Hannah heard the broadcast about the missing children and put two and two together. We may be on a wild goose chase, but if you're game—"

"You mean a wild horse chase!" George chimed in. "Okay, Nancy, let's go. But where to?"

"I wish I knew," Nancy replied. "Just keep your sharp eyes open."

She drove for several miles into the country before they saw a barn that appeared deserted.

"Look!" cried George. "A hex sign with a flaming red horse."

Nancy stopped the car behind some bushes near the

entrance to a weed-filled driveway. "We'd better walk in," she said.

As they neared the old barn the girls became aware of voices inside. "I don't want to go to the lake. I want to go home!" cried a high-pitched voice. I wonder if it's a child's, Nancy thought.

Nancy and George quietly sneaked up to a side door of the old barn. They were just in time to see two men and a woman. One man was holding a little girl, who was struggling to get away. The other man, dark-haired and heavy-set, carried a boy, who was kicking and punching his captor.

"Stop that, you brat!" the man commanded, but the boy did not obey.

"Help! Help!" the little girl cried out.

The two men, grasping the children tightly, rushed out the big front door of the barn toward a waiting dark-colored station wagon. They put the boy and girl in the back, then jumped into the front seat. The woman had gone ahead, started the car, and now sent it roaring off.

"Quick!" Nancy exclaimed. "Let's go!"

She and George raced back to her car and in seconds were following the station wagon along the country road. Suddenly Nancy groaned. Her convertible was slowing down. The needle on the gas gauge pointed to EMPTY. As the engine finally died, Nancy turned the car off the road.

While this was going on, George kept her eyes focused on the fleeing station wagon. At a fork in the road just ahead it took the branch to the left and disappeared.

"Rotten luck, Nancy, and we never got close enough to get the license number," George exclaimed. "If only we knew where they were headed. Those poor children. That gas gauge must have been stuck. It registered almost full when we started."

"I know," Nancy replied with concern. "We've got to track those people down somehow. I guess now my only chance is seeing the ghost jogger tonight in the park."

George stepped out of the car and waved down an oncoming truck. The kindly driver offered to stop at a service station. There he arranged for an attendant to bring back a can of gasoline to the girls, which he did promptly, poured the fuel into the thirsty tank, then left.

At the first opportunity they called the police with the information. But as Nancy suspected, with nothing but the station wagon as a lead, there was little hope of finding the children.

This time George took the wheel and soon was pulling up in front of her house. "Call me later, Nancy, and let me know what happens—and be careful!"

"I promise," Nancy replied, moving over to the driver's seat to head home.

Once there, she quickly changed into her warm-up suit and by seven o'clock was down at the park. The weather had turned cool and it was now drizzling.

Nancy found it uncomfortable just standing around looking at the runners' faces, so she decided to jog. She had made two trips around the cinder track before the ghost jogger appeared. He was wearing the same long white raincoat and hood. He quickened his pace to reach her and suddenly, a hand shot out again holding a note. Nancy slowed down and opened it.

THANK YOU FOR YOUR HARD WORK. TOO BAD IT
ENDED THE WAY IT DID. NOW TRY THE RIVERBOAT
WITH THE OLD SEA CAPTAIN!

Nancy turned her head to ask her jogging companion a question, but he was gone as quickly as he had appeared!

Where? How? Nancy looked ahead, behind her, and to each side. He was not in sight. Nancy was mystified. There was no place anyone could hide. Even in the dusk, the white cape should have been spotted easily if it were anywhere nearby.

Oh, dear, Nancy thought. I guess I'll have to follow his instructions and not worry now about the identity of the "family ghost."

She again called the police, but they obviously felt it was all too vague for them to follow up.

At home later she told her father the whole strange story, then asked him, "Dad, did you ever hear of a boat on our river run by an old sea captain?"

Mr. Drew thought for several moments, then replied, "I seem to recall a story about a reclusive sea captain who docked his boat in the River Heights dock a long time ago. He was supposed to be quite a character."

"Is he still alive?" Nancy broke in.

Mr. Drew shook his head uncertainly. "I heard that a year or two ago the ship and its captain disappeared. It was thought he might have tried to get back to the Gulf."

Nancy asked, "What kind of ship was it?"

"I believe it was a steamer—called the *Magnolia*."

"I wonder what the connection is between the ghost jogger's message and the riverboat and captain. One thing's for sure, there's no time to waste if those children are to be rescued, but I can't do it in the dark."

Nancy phoned Bess and George. "Better eat a good breakfast tomorrow morning," she warned them. "We have some important sleuthing to do for those missing children!"

"Let's jog before we go," George suggested.

"Good idea," Nancy replied. "We can't afford to miss a chance to run with the family ghost. He may appear during the day as well as the night. I'll pick you up about seven A.M."

To the girls' disappointment the mysterious figure did not appear while they were at the track.

"I'm likely to lose some weight if we keep this up," Bess panted as they left the park.

"Marvin, the skeleton," George kidded her cousin, then reported that she had heard on a TV newscast that there was no new word about the missing children.

"If the police can't find them, what chance do we have?" Bess complained.

"You forget how we earned our fantastic reputation," George countered. "We have spirit and determination!"

"And we have Nancy!" Bess reminded her with a laugh.

As the three girls approached the river in Nancy's car, George asked the young detective where she expected to pick up a clue.

"From a native riverman," Nancy replied. "Ned went camping once on Tall Tree Island and met a man named Pete who knows everything about the Muskoka River. We'll try to track him down."

"How are we going to get there?" George asked. "Swim?"

"I have a big surprise," was the answer, as she parked the car. "Follow me!"

Nancy led the way to a boat rental dock and pointed to a sleek, maroon speedboat with white lettering that spelled *Discoverer*.

"Isn't she a beauty?" Nancy exclaimed.

"Don't tell me," Bess remarked. "Let me guess. Your father bought it for you yesterday!"

Nancy laughed. "Not quite, but he did rent if for a month or two, intending to use it for fun on the weekends."

"She sure is gorgeous," George agreed. "And are we going to Florida in this?"

Nancy enjoyed George's humor. "Not yet. Only to Tall Tree Island. All aboard, mates!"

The girls climbed in the sleek craft and soon the *Discoverer* was speeding across the river with Nancy at the wheel.

"Smooth as silk," Bess approved.

"I just wish we were on a pleasure trip instead of a search for lost children," George admitted.

The others agreed.

Following Ned's directions, Nancy reached the small land mass with a coast of low trees. Just one tall pine rose from the center. At the edge of the group of trees stood a dock and small shack. A hound lay asleep in front of it, but at the sound of the *Discoverer's* motor, the dog raised his head, blinked one eye, stood up and gave a deep, throaty *woof*.

Instantly the door opened. A tall, thin man with oversized hands and feet stepped outside and shook his head as if he had just awakened. His wispy blond-gray hair swung from side to side, then settled into place.

"Some welcoming committee," Bess whispered with a grin.

"Good morning," Nancy said. "I'm sorry to bother you, but are you Pete, the famous riverman?"

"That I am," he replied, a smile turning up his mouth. "And you're no bother, either. Gets kinda lonely 'round here with just Sailor and me." He patted the old hound affectionately. "Now, what can I do for you?"

"I've been told," the girl detective replied, "that you

could tell me about the legendary lost ship *Magnolia*."

"She ain't lost," Pete said quickly. "There's not a word o' truth to that rumor. Certain folks just don't want her whereabouts to be known."

"Why?"

"I dunno. Say, I wonder what shape the *Magnolia*'s in these days. Rats and squirrels and birds coulda made a mess o' that fine little steamer."

"I wish we could find out," Nancy urged. "Is there any chance you could take us to her today?"

Pete noted the three girls' eager expressions. "Adventure-lovers, eh?" he said with a grin. "I don't see why I can't," he continued, "but why don't you ladies sit down for a spell and we'll have a bite to eat before we set out."

Bess, especially, was happy with this suggestion. Soon the foursome were enjoying a cool drink and fresh fruit, while Nancy told Pete the purpose of their search.

After the riverman tied his hound to a post, he put on a battered felt hat. Then he and the girls climbed into the *Discoverer* and headed downriver. A mile farther on Pete directed Nancy to enter a shadowy inlet.

She was a bit apprehensive. "Is this safe?" she asked him. "How about tree roots or logs in the water that could foul up the *Discoverer*?"

"If we keep in the channel we'll be all right," Pete said, directing her carefully. Ten minutes later he called out, "Look ahead! Thar she be!"

The girls stared. Moored to one side of the tree-lined riverbank was a small steamer. It had been painted white, but now most of the paint had chipped off and it looked like a forlorn derelict.

Bess spoke up. "I thought nobody lived on it. I think I see a light."

"That's mighty odd," Pete replied. "We'd better see who's aboard." Cupping his hands to his mouth, as the *Discoverer* drifted towards the steamer, he shouted, "Ship ahoy, *Magnolia*!"

No one appeared on deck, but a stentorian voice boomed out, "Come any closer and you'll regret it!"

Bess was trembling. "Oh, Pete, let's go back," she pleaded.

"Not yet," said George. "It's just getting interesting!"

Suddenly there was a scream inside the steamer. It was followed by a child's voice. "Let go of me! I don't want to stay here with you! I want to go home!"

The girls stared at one another. Was this one of the missing children? Should Nancy and her small rescue party board the boat?

"It's too dangerous," Bess declared. "Someone in the steamer might harm them—and us, too."

Pete held up his hand to caution them. "Hold fast," he said. "You girls wait here. I'll go aboard and find out what's goin' on."

His offer came too late. Nancy was already quietly climbing up a rope ladder on the side of the *Magnolia*. She had almost reached an opening into the hold of the steamer when a man wearing a sea captain's uniform leaned over the railing and ordered her to stop.

"What do you think you're doing?" he shouted. "Stay away from here!"

Instead of obeying, she disappeared into the hold as a metal door dropped into place behind her.

I must get out of here fast, Nancy realized. Feeling around the walls in semi-darkness, she hunted for an inside door. The air was very heavy, which made it difficult for Nancy to breathe. She kept searching, however, and just as she was about to faint, her fingers felt a wooden bar.

Nancy lifted it and a heavy door swung open silently. Beyond stretched a corridor with several staterooms. The crew's quarters, no doubt.

The excited young detective took several deep breaths of the fresher air, then scooted along the corridor to a stairway at the end.

Just before reaching it, Nancy heard the children again. "I won't go!" one screamed. The other cried out, "Mommy! Daddy! Where are you? Come and get us!"

Nancy did not hesitate. She bounded up the steps into a galley, raced through a small dining area and into a lounge. She was just in time to see a small boy and girl carried out by two men. She raced after them into a narrow corridor that had an opening on one side with steps down to the water. The kidnappers were already halfway down the stairs.

Suddenly Nancy felt a presence behind her. Turning her head slightly, she caught a glimpse of white. The ghost jogger!

"Get your boat and follow me to the old boathouse," he whispered.

She debated a few seconds whether to obey or continue after the abductors, as the children were still screaming to be freed. Nancy decided she had better get some help.

She turned and speedily retraced her steps through the *Magnolia* to the outer door of the hold. To her relief, Pete stood in the opening, having reopened the door.

The two hurried down the rope ladder and jumped into the *Discoverer*. The girl detective quickly explained the situation while George kept the motor running. Pete took the wheel and sent the boat to the other side of the steamer.

Disappearing down the inlet was the kidnappers' boat, with the ghost not far behind in another speedboat. Peter revved up the motor of the *Discoverer*, which then gradually caught up to the fleeing craft.

A race began down the inlet, with the ghost's boat and Nancy's side by side. She shouted across, "Who has the children?"

"My Uncle John Clark. He's determined to get some ransom money."

"Who kidnapped the children?" Nancy asked.

"I think he did or his pals."

Nancy was confused.

"We mustn't let Uncle John carry out his plan," and

get away with all that money," the ghost continued. "We must stop him!"

Nancy responded to the urgency of the situation immediately. "Pete, please can this boat go any faster? We must stay close!" she cried out.

As the ghost boat shot ahead, the riverman speeded up the Discoverer. A few minutes later, the craft ahead turned sharply to the left and entered a large old boathouse.

As Pete followed, a corrugated metal door slammed down, landing just back of the cockpit. Nancy and Peter were cut off from Bess and George! They all tried to raise the door but in vain.

"Well, what now?" Pete asked.

"I'm going to investigate this building," Nancy said. "If I'm not back in fifteen minutes, come and get me."

She crawled across the flat prow of the Discoverer onto the aft deck of the ghost's boat. The jogger had already left.

Alongside his boat lay the kidnappers' craft. No one was aboard. Apparently, the children had been taken to the apartment on the second floor of the boathouse.

There was not a sound until a board overhead creaked. It was followed by a man's stern command: "Stop where you are! You can't scare me, you phony ghost!"

"Not so phony now," the other replied. "You nicknamed me the family ghost because I was always appearing when you didn't want me to. It's a good thing I did."

"Uncle John Clark, your deceitful game is up!" the

young man added. "You'll never get the ransom money."

"And who's to stop me?" Mr. Clark snarled. "You forget, I have the children."

"But we want to go home," a child's voice cried out.

Nancy spotted a stairway leading upward and noiselessly ascended it. Quickly she tried to formulate a plan to rescue the children safely. Was there time? She would need the ghost to help her. Of that she was sure.

Reaching the apartment, Nancy found herself in a tiny kitchen. Adjoining it was another small room with a wooden door made only of heavy, crisscrossed slats. Through the openings she could see the boy and girl. They shrank back upon seeing Nancy and were beginning to cry.

The girl detective put a finger to her lips, then smiled. "I've come to save you," she whispered to the youngsters soothingly. "Please don't be afraid."

"This door's locked," the trembling boy explained quietly.

Nancy looked around carefully. She noticed a sturdy bar across the door on the outside and swung it back.

"Come on! Follow me!" she directed the children, stretching out her arms.

She led the way down the stairs. To her delight, Pete had managed to raise the metal door of the boathouse. In seconds, Nancy and the two young children had climbed over to the *Discoverer*, where

Bess and George were waiting when heavy footsteps clattered down the boathouse steps.

"Pete, take off!" Nancy ordered.

Before he could back out, however, they heard a loud-sounding horn, and a Coast Guard patrol boat pulled into the boathouse behind the *Discoverer* and stopped abruptly. Two lieutenants stood up. A man and a woman behind them also stood up and exclaimed, "Our children! Tom! Sally! You're all right!"

Startled, the brother and sister looked back, then cried out, "Mommy! Daddy!"

As the children started to scramble from one boat to the other, a heavyset man appeared at the foot of the stairway and shouted, "Stop! You can't take those children until you pay me the reward money. I found them!"

"You didn't *find* them, you *kidnapped* them," another voice accused him angrily. "Uncle John, you're an abductor and almost a thief as well!"

The ghost! Only his hood was down now, and Nancy could see he was a rather handsome young man. He was standing up in his own boat. Turning toward the children's parents, he said, "Don't give Uncle John a nickel. I overheard him talking to his cronies and learned they had kidnapped the children. I promised myself right then and there that he wouldn't get away with it. But I just couldn't call the police. After all, he is my uncle and I was so afraid of a family scandal, I knew he would never actually harm the children. So I decided to get Nancy Drew's help. I was afraid he'd figure out I was on to him, and so I couldn't contact her out in the open. I had to wear a disguise. I didn't want her to know who I was either, and hoped she'd fall for my act. I was right to enlist her help. She's the best girl detective on land—or sea!"

At that moment one of the Coast Guard lieutenants spoke up. "Miss Drew, your father became worried about you and your friends. When he called and told us of your riverman clue, we figured we'd better come out to find you. It's lucky we all know old Pete, here, and are familiar with the landmarks in these waters."

Mr. Clark and his accomplices stood in disgusted silence as the police took them into custody for later questioning. The triumphant "ghost" watched as the children were happily reunited with their parents.

Tom and Sally called in loud voices, "Three cheers for Nancy Drew and her friends!"

Nancy smiled at Bess and George, then saluted their riverman friend.

"We wouldn't have this happy ending without our experienced captain, Pete. He helped the *Discoverer* really live up to its name!"

The Curse of the Frog

"**M**adame Zurga terrifies people who come to have their fortunes told, Nancy! They think she's a witch. She frightens them so badly, they'll do whatever she tells them to!"

Nancy Drew listened sympathetically to the gypsy girl seated across the table from her in the Romany Tearoom. Mary Lukash had on gold earrings, a kerchief tied around her head, a long colorful skirt, and tinkly bracelets and necklaces. She spoke and behaved however like any other American teenager.

"What exactly do you want me to do, Mary?" asked the reddish-blond-haired detective.

"You're so good at solving mysteries, Nancy! Can't you expose Madame Zurga's trickery? If you don't, I'm afraid she'll give all the gypsies around here a bad name with the police!"

"Can't your own people do anything about her?"

Mary Lukash sadly shook her head, her long blue-black hair swaying about her shoulders. "No, they're almost as much afraid of her as her customers are. When the chief of our tribe ordered her to stop scaring and cheating people, she just sneered and threatened to put the frog curse on him! He has no power over her."

"The frog curse?" Nancy stared in surprise at the gypsy girl. "What's that?"

"I'm not sure myself. All I can tell you is that Madame Zurga has a strange frog with some sort of weird powers. Even gypsies who've seen it come away scared out of their wits. They're convinced it's possessed by an evil spirit that can haunt them and cause terrible tragedy!"

Mary explained that Madame Zurga belonged to a different tribe of gypsies from her own. She had opened her fortune-telling parlor in River Heights only recently.

Nancy already knew that such fortune-tellers sometimes plied their skill at bajour—or what police called "the badger game"—as a way to trick their clients out of money while pretending to offer them help with their personal problems.

"But many gypsies here in town believe that Madame Zurga's frog is a demon in animal form, sent by the devil himself," Mary went on. "They say she could never have learned from our own Romany people how to tame such an evil creature!"

Nancy Drew continued talking for a while with her friend in the tearoom, which was owned by Mary's

108

parents. She learned that gypsies originally came from India centuries ago and still speak a language called Romany, which is related to the ancient Indian tongue, Sanskrit.

As these people wandered about the world, they supported themselves by their skills at metalworking, as well as in horse trading and animal doctoring. In the Middle Ages, most people thought they were from Egypt, so they became known as gypsies.

Nowadays, Mary told Nancy, American gypsies are more apt to drive vans or station wagons than to ride about in horse-drawn caravans. Many have settled down to work at house painting or driveway paving or selling used cars. Some hold professional positions. But others still prefer to keep on the move.

"What delicious tea!" Nancy said as she sipped the last fragrant cup from the pot.

Mary smiled proudly. "My mother blends it with herbs and flavorings known only to gypsies."

Rising to go, Nancy promised to investigate Madame Zurga. "I'm not sure anyone can stop her from telling fortunes," Nancy informed the gypsy girl. "But I'll certainly try to find out how she frightens people so badly with her weird 'frog curse.' She can't be allowed to scare people out of their money."

Outside the tearoom, Nancy took the wheel of her blue sports car. Only four o'clock, she noted, glancing at her wristwatch. That should give me time enough to visit Madame Zurga before dinner.

The fortune-telling parlor was located in what had

once been a store, across the street from Riverview Park. A sign on the curtained window read: MA-DAME ZURGA, ORIENTAL PALMIST, CRYSTAL-GAZER & SPIRITUAL ADVISER.

Below that, another sign advised passersby to CON-SULT MADAME ZURGA ABOUT ALL YOUR PERSONAL PROB-LEMS!

She certainly has confidence in her own powers, Nancy thought, repressing a wry smile. That "all" could take in everything from how to pay your bills to overcoming shyness—or clearing up warts!

A gong sounded in the back of the store as she entered. Nancy found herself in a small, bare room furnished only with a folding chair and a painting on the wall of a beautiful gypsy woman with a mysterious light shining all around her head.

Nancy sat down to wait. As her gaze flickered about the room, she noticed the eyes of the gypsy woman in the picture moved slightly. Again the young detective tried not to smile. She realized that Madame Zurga was studying her latest client.

Presently a voice spoke over a concealed intercom: "You may now enter the spiritual chamber!" It was a woman's voice, but powerful and hypnotic and almost as deep as a man's.

Nancy got up and went through a curtained door-way into a back room. Its walls were hung with dark purple drapes which seemed to muffle sound. In the center of the room were two chairs and a small table bearing a crystal ball. A burning cone of incense by a wall stand filled the chamber with a strange scent.

The Curse of the Frog

But what caught Nancy's interest at once was a large green frog. It was perched on the table near the crystal ball. Its bulging eyes glared at her with a sinister intensity.

This must be the frog Mary Lukash told me about, Nancy thought. At first the creature seemed so real she assumed it was alive. But when it remained motionless, Nancy realized the frog was only a stuffed one, prepared by a skilled taxidermist.

Nevertheless, she pulled her chair safely away from the repulsive green creature before sitting down. Her head was beginning to ache, and the room seemed to waver before her eyes.

The incense fumes must be making me woozy, Nancy reflected in annoyance.

Oriental music began to play. Almost as if the gypsy fortune-teller had read the girl's mind, the air gradually seemed to clear. But Nancy's headache did not go away.

The curtains parted, and Madame Zurga entered the chamber. The fortune-teller was a tall, imposing woman with a beak nose, glowing dark eyes, and heavy black brows. She was dressed in gypsy fashion with a colorful kerchief on her head, a long green-and-yellow gown, and golden bangles, necklace, and earrings.

"Good afternoon, Miss Drew," she intoned, seating herself across the table.

Nancy blinked in amazement. How did Madame Zurga know her name? Was it possible that the fortune-teller really did have occult powers?

111

"Hold the frog in your two hands," the gypsy woman ordered.

Nancy's skin crawled at the thought of touching the slimy object. She tried to protest, yet somehow the right words failed to come to her lips.

"Pick up the frog!" Madame Zurga insisted sharply. "Its magical vibrations help me peer into the future and foresee what life holds for you!"

Nancy found herself meekly obeying. The swarthy gypsy woman began to chant eerily in a strange language which Nancy guessed must be Romany.

Suddenly Nancy's heart skipped a beat. The frog seemed to be coming alive in her hands! She could feel its throat throbbing in and out. It was actually croaking! *Glup! . . . Glup! . . . Glup!*

Nancy wanted to drop the creature like a hot coal. But Madame Zurga's dark eyes fixed her with a piercing glare. "Do not let go of the frog!" she hissed, "or its curse will strike you!"

The gypsy's gaze returned to her crystal ball. "I see grave trouble ahead . . . for both you and your father," she droned. "He is an attorney, is he not?"

Again her eyes drilled into those of the young detective. Nancy nodded.

"Some unknown enemy is plotting against you—I can sense his evil power!" Madame Zurga declared. "The trouble has to do with your father's law practice. What important cases is he handling?"

"I—I c-c-can't tell you," Nancy mumbled. "L-lawyers aren't allowed to d-discuss their clients' af-f-fairs with outsiders!"

"Wait!" the gypsy exclaimed. "I see the trouble now. Your enemy has placed a curse on something in your father's office safe. It must be removed at once, or you both may die! Only I can save you from such a curse. Tell me! What is the combination to his safe?"

Nancy's brain was in a whirl. She could not seem to focus her thoughts. Nevertheless, she sensed that if she stayed in Madame Zurga's fortune-telling parlor any longer, she might give up all sorts of private family information!

But was she brave enough to defy the gypsy woman's threatened curse?

Nancy let go of the frog and stood up. Plucking some money from her purse, she dropped it on the table and hurried out of the purple-draped chamber.

Behind her, she heard an angry outburst from Madame Zurga, ordering her to remain. The commands were followed by a sneering laugh when the gypsy saw that her teenage client had no intention of obeying.

Outside, Nancy took a deep breath of fresh air. Then she walked across the street into Riverview Park. Stopping at a refreshment stand, she bought some orangeade. A few swallows of the ice-cold drink helped to clear her head. She was feeling much better now.

Whatever came over me? Nancy wondered. When she fled from the fortune-telling parlor, she had found herself halfway believing that Madame Zurga really possessed occult powers or second sight.

But now, bit by bit, it was all becoming clear . . .

How had the gypsy known her name, or the fact that her father was a lawyer? Nothing very surprising about that. Nancy's picture often appeared in the paper, in connection with the mysteries she solved. Madame Zurga had simply recognized her.

No doubt the incense gave off some sort of anesthetic fumes. When customers inhaled the vapor, it left them too giddy and confused to hold back any secrets from the gypsy fortune-teller. No wonder Nancy had felt so woozy!

The Oriental music probably covered the sound of an exhaust fan which drew off the fumes and cleared the air before Madame Zurga made her appearance.

But what about the frog? In her imagination, Nancy could still feel the horrid creature breathing in and out, and hear its ominous croaking!

"Oh, Nancy!" a voice called out.

The young sleuth turned and saw a school friend named Nicole Lamar hurrying toward her. "Hi, Nikki! Where did you come from?"

"Across the street." Nicole seemed a bit breathless. "Didn't I just see you coming out of Madame Zurga's fortune-telling parlor?"

Nancy nodded, smiling ruefully. "Mary Lukash suspects the woman is running a racket that may get all the local gypsies in trouble with the law. So she asked me to expose her, but I almost got victimized myself!"

"Oh, Nancy, did you really? That's exactly what I wanted to talk to you about!"

Nicole was an orphan, who lived with her unmarried cousin, Yvette Lamar. She related that Ms. Lamar had long bccn a fan of fortune-tellers. So when Madame Zurga opened her parlor in River Heights, Yvette had immediately gone to consult her.

"When my cousin got home that evening, I could see she was upset and frightened," Nikki went on, "but she wouldn't tell me what was wrong. Then, a few days later, she went to see Madame Zurga again, and came home looking even worse. Since then, she's been going to Madame Zurga's fortune-telling parlor two or three times a week and it's turning her into a nervous wreck!"

"Do you know what she consults Madame Zurga about?" asked Nancy.

Nicole shook her head. "Not really. At first I think she went mostly in fun. Cousin Yvette just likes to hear fortune-tellers predict what will happen to her next week or next year, and whether she may take a long trip or meet a man she could fall in love with and marry. But Madame Zurga must had told her something that really scared her! Somehow I have a feeling it's connected with the past."

Nancy knit her brows. "But you have no idea what it is she's afraid of?"

Nikki hesitated. "This is just a guess, but . . . would you laugh if I said Cousin Yvette seems to think she's being haunted?"

"Of course not. That doesn't mean I believe in ghosts myself, Nikki, but a lot of people do."

"Well, here's something else that may sound even sillier. She seems to have an absolute *phobia* about frogs! We were strolling along the riverbank yesterday evening about sunset, near the marshes, when a frog suddenly began croaking. Cousin Yvette was so scared, she almost jumped out of her skin!"

Nancy smiled grimly. "That doesn't surprise me." She described the frog Madame Zurga uses to frighten her clients. Nikki shuddered upon hearing how the creature seemed to breathe and croak when held.

"Oh, Nancy! Please do me a favor," she begged. "Today's Friday. Would you come and stay with me over the weekend, and see if you can find out what's troubling Cousin Yvette?"

Nancy felt sure that Ms. Lamar's problem must be connected with Madame Zurga's fortune-telling scam. Clearing up one mystery might help to solve the other as well.

"All right," she agreed. "Come home with me first while I pack some things and tell Hannah. Then I'll drive us to your place."

Nikki and her cousin lived in a comfortable old stone house on the outskirts of River Heights. Nancy had already met Yvette Lamar. She was a kindly, attractive woman in her late forties, but now her face showed signs of strain and sleeplessness.

Over dinner that evening, Nancy drew Ms. Lamar into conversation about her background. "Nikki says you come from the Island of Martinique in the West Indies," she remarked.

"Yes, I lived there with my uncle when I was a little girl," Yvette replied. "He was a sailor and fisherman. He took me in and cared for me after my parents died. Then when I was seven or eight, we moved to the United States. He became a ship chandler and did well enough in business to build this house before he retired."

The Lamar family, she added, was originally from Alabama. But her great-grandfather, a Confederate colonel, had gone to the West Indies after the Civil War. Over the years, his descendants had moved back to the United States, one by one. "My Uncle Louis was the last one in the family to do so."

"Lucky for me he did!" said Nikki with a smile. Jumping up from her chair, she gave the middle-aged woman a fond hug before clearing off the main-course dishes to make way for dessert.

Later, when dinner was over and the two girls had helped Cousin Yvette load the dishwasher, all three settled down in the oak-beamed living room to chat and watch television.

"What a lovely fireplace!" Nancy exclaimed.

"My uncle built it himself," said Yvette. "He was a jack-of-all-trades and would have been a good stone mason. He even carved that ship design in some of the stones."

Soon after eleven o'clock, they retired for the night. Nancy's room was directly across the hall from Nicole's. After changing, the two girls talked a while longer as they brushed their hair before going to bed.

Settling down in her own room, Nancy read for a few minutes. When she felt herself getting drowsy, she turned off the light.

It seemed to Nancy as if she had hardly drifted off to sleep when she awoke with a start. A scream echoed throughout the house!

Nancy sprang out of bed and pulled on a robe. Nikki was already poking her head out of her own doorway. She looked pale and frightened.

"That was Cousin Yvette!" she gasped.

"Where's her room?" Nancy asked.

"On the other side of the house."

Just then another faint scream was heard!

"Come on! Let's find out what's wrong!" Nancy urged.

Together the two girls ran to Ms. Lamar's room, Nikki pointing the way. A muffled croak came from somewhere inside. Nancy knocked hastily, then flung open the door.

Cousin Yvette was sitting upright in bed, big-eyed with fear. "L-l-look!" she quavered, and with a trembling hand pointed to the window.

The ghostly, glowing apparition of a frog could be seen on the window curtain!

Another croak reverberated, then another and another. *Glup. . . . Glup. . . . Glup.*

It sounded exactly like the repulsive frog in Madame Zurga's fortune-telling parlor!

The two girls stood totally still, shocked by the vision. But Nancy quickly snapped out of her trance and ran to the window.

As she did so, the ghostly frog faded from view. Nancy pulled aside the curtain and peered out into the darkness. Nothing seemed to be moving on the grounds or in the garden. All that was visible were the moonlit forms of trees and shrubbery.

Nancy turned back from the window and saw that Cousin Yvette was still shaking with fright.

"Let's make some cocoa," Nancy said to Nicole. "Then we can talk about what happened."

By the time all three were seated in the bright, cozy living room, sipping their hot drinks, the girls' mood had become more cheerful. Even Cousin Yvette seemed to take heart from Nancy's calm, matter-of-fact manner.

"Were we all just imagining things?" Yvette asked.

Nancy shook her head. "No, we did hear croaks, and that glowing frog did appear in your window. But I doubt that it was a ghost or anything else supernatural."

"Then what were we seeing?"

"I'm not sure. I have a vague idea, but there's no use discussing it until it can be checked out." Nancy hesitated, then said, "Tell me, have you always been afraid of frogs?"

Ms. Lamar frowned and passed a hand over her forehead. "I . . . I don't really know. Perhaps something happened once that made them seem unpleasant. I guess I just never thought about it until . . . until I went to see a fortune-teller recently."

"Madame Zurga?"

119

"Yes!" On learning that Nancy too had visited the gypsy woman and handled the weird frog, Cousin Yvette seemed relieved and willing to talk more freely. "It was right after I started going to Madame Zurga," she related, "that I began having nightmares and seeing that horrible frog."

"Then tonight wasn't the first time?" Nancy inquired.

"Oh, no! I keep seeing the frog and hearing it croak night after night!"

"Has Madame Zurga offered to help you?"

"Yes, but mostly she just asks me questions . . . about my past life, and especially about my Uncle Louis."

Ms. Lamar said that, although she was only a small child at the time, she remembered that when they had moved from the West Indies to the United States, her uncle had seemed worried and fearful, as if afraid some terrible misfortune might befall them.

"But none ever did?" Nancy asked.

"Far from it. His business prospered and our life was very happy. But during his final illness, he started worrying again.

"Just before he died," Cousin Yvette continued, "my uncle murmured, 'Seven stones tell the truth. But it is better that my secret remain bottled up forever!' "

Nancy and Nikki exchanged puzzled looks.

"Did you tell that to Madame Zurga?" Nancy asked.

"Yes, and I also gave her a bottle of stones." Ms.

120

Lamar explained that after her uncle passed away, she had found the bottle on his closet shelf. It contained exactly seven stones.

"They look like ordinary pebbles to me," she went on. "But I kept them, anyhow. When I gave them to Madame Zurga, I didn't think she could discover anything special about them. At any rate, she keeps telling me that if I want to save myself from the 'Curse of the Frog,' I must find out my uncle's secret and tell it to her."

There was a brief silence. Nikki had kindled a small fire behind the grate to ward off the night's chill. Nancy gazed thoughtfully into the flickering flames while she tried to unravel the mystery. As she turned back to face her two companions, she gave a sudden start.

"Your uncle mentioned *seven* stones?" she asked.

"Yes. Why?"

Nancy pointed to the fireplace. "There are exactly seven of those stones that your Uncle Louis carved a ship on!"

Both Cousin Yvette and Nikki were startled by the odd coincidence. But neither they nor the girl detective could figure out what it might mean. The stones were arranged like an upside-down V enclosing the fireplace opening. When Nancy tested them, she found that all were firmly mortared in place and could not be moved.

Next morning, directly after breakfast, the doorbell rang. Nikki went to answer. A few moments later she ushered a tall, craggy-faced man with brush-cut iron-gray hair into the room. He held his hat in one hand and had a camera slung around his neck.

Nikki introduced him. "This is Mr. Karnak. He writes pieces for an interior decoration magazine, and would like to do a feature story on your fireplace, Cousin Yvette."

"Someone told our editor about it," he explained, "and mentioned the beautiful hand-carved stones. Do you mind if I photograph them?" As he spoke, his eyes were busy studying the carvings.

Ms. Lamar readily gave permission. Mr. Karnak snapped a number of pictures, moving closer and closer to the fireplace as he did so.

When he finished photographing, he took out a small penknife and tried to insert the blade around the edges of one of the carved stones.

Nancy, who had been watching all this with a slight frown, suddenly spoke up. "What are you doing, Mr. Karnak?"

"Just, er, seeing if any of the stones are loose. I thought Ms. Lamar might let me take them to my studio, so I could photograph them close-up in better lighting."

"Wouldn't it be more polite to ask her permission before you scrape away any of the mortar?" As the man's gaze flickered uncertainly toward Ms. Lamar, Nancy went on, "In any case, I can tell you the stones aren't loose and don't come out. What magazine did you say you write for, Mr. Karnak?"

"I didn't say."

"Then would you care to tell us now? And also who mentioned the fireplace to your editor?"

The visitor's expression hardened nastily. "You don't seem to trust me, young lady. I've been a writer for years, and I certainly don't have to show you my credentials!"

Turning to his hostess, he added huffily, "If I'm intruding where I'm not wanted, Ms. Lamar, please forgive me!"

Without another word, Karnak stalked out of the room and left the house. Nancy and Nikki watched from the window as he drove away.

Nancy had spoken on the spur of the moment, and the incident left her a bit upset. "Please forgive me if I spoke out of turn," she said to her hostess. "Somehow I don't trust that man."

"Don't worry, dear, I'm glad you questioned him as you did," Ms. Lamar assured her. "In my opinion, you took exactly the right tone. One can't be too careful of strangers these days!"

After an early lunch, Nancy excused herself for an hour or two. She explained that she had to shop for a gift for a friend's three-year-old child. "I'd ask you to come with me, Nikki," she added privately, "but after that queer visit from Mr. Karnak, I think it might be best not to leave your cousin here alone."

Toward evening, it began to rain and the wind rose. After dinner, Cousin Yvette and the two girls gathered in front of the fireplace. Yvette described a thrilling rescue at sea which her uncle had once told her about.

"If only I knew the secret that worried him all those years." She sighed. "Somehow I feel that's the key to whatever is haunting this house."

"Is his room still the way it was when he died?" Nancy asked.

"Yes, everything's exactly as he left it. Would you like to see for yourself?"

"Very much. We might find a clue."

The big, chintz-curtained bedroom clearly bespoke a seafaring man. In the closet hung a broad-brimmed sou'wester hat and oilskins; a brass-bound telescope stood on a worktable near the windows; and on the dresser lay several scrimshawed ivory knickknacks.

Gazing about the room, Nancy ran over Louis Lamar's last words in her mind: *"Seven stones tell the truth. But it is better that my secret remain bottled up forever!"*

A *bottle!* Her eyes had just fallen on a hand-crafted toy vessel in a bottle. The vessel was a two-masted schooner. Nancy walked over to examine it more closely. Every bit of canvas, cordage, and other details were scaled to size, evidently by a loving hand. Then she noticed the schooner's name, painted in tiny gold letters on the stern counter: *La Grenouille.*

Nancy gasped excitedly and looked at Ms. Lamar. "Do you speak French?"

"I used to, but I'm afraid I've forgotten most of it. Why?"

"This schooner is named *The Frog!*"

Cousin Yvette's eyes widened, and her faced drained of color. She clapped both hands to her cheeks and sank down heavily on the crazy-quilted bed. "Oh no!" she murmured in a shocked voice. "*Now* I remember!"

"Remember what?" asked Nikki.

"Why frogs seem so dreadful to me!" Yvette related that once when she was a little girl in the West Indies, she had gone looking for her uncle along the beach one evening. Spying a glimmer of light from a cave overlooking the sea, she peered inside. To her horror, she saw a group of men with heads like frogs, squatting around a fire!

"I was scared to death!" she went on. "Then one of the creatures jumped up and pulled off his frog's head, and I saw that it was my Uncle Louis. He had just been wearing a mask. By then I was crying and screaming. He calmed me down and took me home and warned me I must never ever tell anyone what I'd seen!"

"How weird!" said Nikki with a shudder. "What do you suppose he and his friends were doing?"

Cousin Yvette shrugged weakly. "I can't imagine. But I had nightmares for weeks afterward."

Nancy's brain was whirring quickly, seeking further clues. "Let's go back to the living room," she exclaimed. "I've just had an idea!"

Moments later, pointing to the carved stones of the fireplace, she went on, "You'll notice the vessel in all these carvings is a two-masted schooner just like the one in the bottle."

Nicole nodded. "You're right—but so what?"

"The seven stones are arranged like an arrowhead

pointing upward. I'm wondering what they point to." Nancy ran her fingers upward from the topmost stone—then stopped just below the mantel. "Wait till I get a flashlight from my car!"

When she returned, Nancy aimed the flashlight so as to dispel the shadow cast by the mantelpiece. Etched on one of the stones with a line so fine it could barely be seen was the outline of a frog!

"And the stone's loose!" Nancy added, pressing it with her fingers. There was a creaking noise. A bookcase on the right of the fireplace suddenly began to swing outward from the wall!

"Look!" Nikki gasped. "There's a stone staircase inside!"

The steps went downward. Hearts beating nervously, the trio set out to explore where they led. Nancy took the lead, followed by Cousin Yvette, with Nikki bringing up the rear.

At the foot of the stairs was a gloomy passageway. Their steps echoed hollowly in the darkness as they walked along. Guided by the flashlight, they made their way to a stone-walled room.

At the far side of the room stood an old sea chest, with a cement frog perched on top of it. On the wall behind the chest hung a pike or boat hook crossed with an old-time sailor's cutlass.

"Oh g-g-goodness!" said Cousin Yvette in a shaky voice. "Dare we open the chest?"

"Why not?" said Nancy boldly. "We came down here to solve the mystery, didn't we?"

With Nikki's help, she lifted off the heavy cement

frog, which had seemed to be protecting the chest like a watchdog. Then they pried open the creaky lid.

The chest was heaped with jewelry! Rings, bracelets, gold watches, necklaces, pearl stickpins—a bewildering variety of valuables!

There was also a folded paper, which Nancy opened and read. Nikki, meanwhile, was fingering through the jewelry. "Where did all this come from?" she asked in an awestruck tone.

"Who cares?" said a harsh voice which Nancy and her two companions had heard earlier that day. "The important thing is you've found it!"

All three looked up and saw Mr. Karnak!

The craggy-faced impostor chuckled as he entered the room, clutching a weapon in one hand. Madame Zurga followed close behind. "How kind of you to unravel Louis Lamar's secret for us, Miss Drew," she taunted. "What a pity you won't be able to enjoy the results of your clever detective work!"

"What makes you think I won't?" Nancy said calmly.

"Because we intend to shut all three of you up in this underground crypt," rasped Karnak. He stooped down to gloat over the treasure, adding, "By the time you're found, if ever, none of you will be alive to tell the police what happened!"

"I'm afraid you're forgetting something," said Nancy.

"Indeed? And what might that be, Miss Busybody?"

Nancy pointed to the passageway, and her voice sank to a fearful hiss: *The Curse of the Frog!*

An ominous croaking resounded through the stone-walled chamber. *Glup! . . . Glup! . . . Glup!*

Karnak stared in open-mouthed disbelief. Madame Zurga clutched her throat with a look of dumbfounded terror. *A huge green frog was hopping toward them!*

With their attention distracted, Nancy seized her chance. She snatched down the pike and cutlass from the wall! "Ned! Catch!" she cried, and tossed them through the air.

Her tall, husky boyfriend, Ned Nickerson, and Burt Eddleton, a fellow member of his college football team, had suddenly appeared out of the darkened passageway. Ned caught the pike, and his pal the cutlass.

Before Karnak could collect his wits and react, Ned swung the pike and knocked the crook's weapon from his hand!

Half an hour later, Karnak and Madame Zurga were seated in the living room with their wrists tied, waiting sullenly for a police car to come and take them away. Ned and Burt, meanwhile, were using an electronic detector to "sweep" the house for eavesdropping bugs.

"I—I still don't understand where that huge frog came from," said Cousin Yvette in bewilderment.

Nancy's eyes twinkled. "I bought it today at a toyshop. Ned stuffed a little tape recorder inside to play the croaking noises."

The tape recorder, she explained, came from a

clump of bushes under Yvette's bedroom window. Inside it was a tape cassette on which amplified frog croaking had been recorded. And a slide projector hidden inside a hollow tree in the garden had beamed the ghostly picture of a frog at her window curtain. "Ned says both the recorder and projector were radio-controlled," Nancy added.

"Wait a second! You're going too fast!" Nikki begged. "How did you discover all this?"

"I guessed last night that this was how the ghostly frog trick was played," Nancy replied. "It was the only possible explanation. So when I went out to shop, I phoned Ned and asked him to come in quietly through the back garden and search for the equipment without disturbing you two."

Karnak's snooping visit, she went on, convinced her that somehow he must have overheard their conversation about the fireplace stones—which meant the house must be "bugged."

"So I knew if we did find out Uncle Louis's secret," Nancy said, "Karnak and Madame Zurga would probably overhear and try to take over. That's why I had Ned prepare the toy frog and stay around to keep watch—so we could use their own trick against them."

Finally, a little more relaxed, Yvette opened the note that had been found in the chest. The letter told where the jewelry came from. As a young man, Yvette's uncle had joined a pirate gang. Wearing frog masks, the gang would attack yachts and cabin cruisers and steal whatever valuables they could find aboard.

Troubled by pangs of guilt, Uncle Louis had finally quit the gang and fled to the United States, taking the loot with him. Stashed at the bottom of the chest was the pirate schooner's log, which contained the names of every boat they had robbed. With this information, Louis Lamar hoped someday to return the stolen jewelry to its rightful owners. But hiding out fearfully from the gang's vengeance, he had never found time or courage to carry out his plan.

At the end of his life, he had half hoped, half feared that his niece Yvette would find and return the loot for him. Therefore he had left her various clues. The bottle of pebbles was a "red herring" to throw off anyone in the gang who might come looking for the treasure.

When the police arrived and questioned Karnak, he sullenly admitted he was the pirate leader's son. Although trained as an electronics engineer, he had spent years trying to track down Louis Lamar.

After finding out Louis was dead, Karnak had learned that his niece Yvette liked to go to fortune-tellers. So he hired Madame Zurga to terrorize her into revealing where the treasure was hidden. He himself had posed as a telephone repairman in order to get into the house and plant the bugs.

"What about Madame Zurga's frog?" asked Nikki, who had listened in fascination while Nancy explained her detective work.

"Well, actually, that she used a frog as a means of tempting everyone was just a coincidence. It's a pretty clever frog too. Ned says it probably contains a heat-sensitive switch," replied Nancy.

Her boyfriend nodded. "That's right. When the frog gets warm from being held in someone's hand, the switch closes. And that's what turns on the mechanism to make it go *glup-glup-glup* . . . at least, that's my guess."

"But if you expect us to go to her fortune-telling parlor tonight and find out for sure—no, thanks!" Nancy added with a smile. "Let's sit here and tell ghost stories!"

The Greenhouse Ghost

"**N**ancy, how would you like to own a little house in the country with a beautiful garden, a swimming pond, a greenhouse—?" Mr. Drew asked his attractive eighteen-year-old daughter, rumpling her reddish blond hair.

"Sounds great, Dad," she replied, "but what's the occasion? It's not my birthday, or Christmas, or . . ."

The tall, athletic-looking lawyer smiled. "Does there have to be an occasion for me to give you a gift?" he countered.

"But this is no ordinary one," Nancy said. Knowing her astute father's knack for teasing, she added, "What's up?"

"Okay," he admitted. "There is such a property for sale, but no one will buy it unless you solve the mystery of the greenhouse ghost."

"Tell me about it," she said eagerly.

Mr. Drew explained that the owner, now deceased, had prided himself on producing the finest orchids in the country. "Nancy, you must have heard of La Forge orchids."

"Oh yes, I have. Brides love them for their wedding bouquets."

"Exactly," the lawyer continued. "Mr. La Forge built up a very prosperous business with his wife. Then suddenly trouble began. A vandal—or vandals—smashed glass, stole or ruined flowers ready to be shipped out, and caused terrible havoc at the estate. Poor Mrs. La Forge died of a sudden heart attack, and her husband passed away soon afterward. I'm co-executor of the estate with the bank. Their children want to sell the property but a rumor that the greenhouse has a ghost keeps people from looking at the place."

"That's a shame," Nancy remarked. "It all sounds very mysterious, but I'm not afraid to go out to the place with you. Let's drive out and meet this ghost!"

Before they could start, Nancy's little dog Togo ran up to her, whimpering and giving staccato barks.

"So you want to go along too," she said, and opened the door of her father's car. At once Togo jumped up and settled himself on the front seat. Nancy climbed in on the passenger's side as Mr. Drew sat down behind the wheel.

On the way, Nancy and her father discussed the raising of orchids. Mr. Drew said that while they grew in several countries with tropical climates, they were first discovered in Malaysia. "That's where Mr. La Forge went to pick out various varieties to bring back here and propagate for commercial use."

"Our florist told me," said Nancy, "that Mr. La Forge was secretly trying to produce a deep blue orchid and guarded his secret well. He'd almost finished working out the formula, when he suddenly died."

"Interesting," Mr. Drew replied. "I heard that too. His children can't find it, though. Oh, look, here we are." He slowed down to enter a shady driveway with stone entrance pillars. On one had been carved the word *Orchidiana*. "That's what the La Forges called this place," the lawyer told Nancy.

The girl detective was charmed by the picturesque gardens of cultivated and wild flowers. When she saw the house, Nancy gasped.

"Dad, you said it was small!" she exclaimed. "Why, it would take a week just to clean the windows!"

Her father explained that the family had used only the center section to live in. One wing was for displaying the orchids. The gardener occupied the other, smaller wing.

As if he had heard his name called, a man came from the left wing. The short, rotund, dark-haired man introduced himself as Joe Hendricks.

"I'm Nancy Drew and this is my father," she said. "What a beautiful place this is. I can't wait to see it all!"

"I'm on my way to the large greenhouse," the gardener said. "Would you like to see that first, or the house?"

Nancy glanced at her father, who nodded.

"I'd like to go to the greenhouse," she said. "Maybe you can tell me something about the ghost."

Hendricks eyed her intently, and his shoulders twitched. He did not reply for several seconds. Regaining his composure, he replied, "Oh, you've heard the story? Don't pay any attention to it. Rumor, that's all. There's no ghost in the greenhouse."

Nancy said no more. She and her father followed the man and presently came to an enormous greenhouse. It was dome-shaped and made entirely of glass. Nancy assumed that the panes shattered by vandals had been replaced.

The visitors followed Hendricks inside. At once, a young man came forward and was introduced by Hendricks as Kiki. "He's my assistant," the gardener explained.

Nancy, who had been in Hawaii some time before, asked Kiki, "Your name sounds Polynesian. Are your ancestors from that area?"

"Yes."

"Tell me," Nancy said, as she and her father followed him down a long aisle between arbors of exquisite dendrobium orchids, "what smells so sweet? Not the orchids?"

"No. We also grow roses and several varieties of lilies," Kiki answered. "They're sold mostly to the local florists."

At the end of the aisle was a door to an enclosed room. On the door hung a sign: NO ADMITTANCE.

"What's in there?" Nancy asked.

"It's an experiment room," Kiki replied, but did not elaborate.

This must be where the secret orchid research was carried on, Nancy thought. How could she find out, yet not seem too curious? Her mind whirled. Was there something else going on in there now? Was it a legitimate business or an undercover operation?

"Nancy, we must go and see the rest of the property," Mr. Drew spoke up. He turned and headed back to the entrance. Nancy followed.

Hendricks and Kiki jumped into a small truck and led the way to the attractive colonial house.

As the group entered, Nancy gasped. A winding stairway stretched upward from a gracious hall. Halfway down from the second floor stood a ghostly figure. It had long straight white hair, a pretty snow-white face, and wore a flowing, tiered white chiffon gown. Its right hand, which was stretched to the side, held a glass tube from which dripped a dark blue fluid.

Hendricks gave a startled gurgle and bolted out the front door, followed by Kiki. Nancy and her father continued to stare. The ghost moved closer to them. Upon reaching the hall, however, it turned, went under the stairway and disappeared.

"Where did it go?" Mr. Drew asked.

Nancy pointed to a door under the stairway, ran to

it, and yanked the door open. The ghost was not there. A stairway led downward.

As Nancy put one foot onto the step below, Mr. Drew grabbed her arm. "No," he said, "you mustn't take chances."

"Oh, Dad, please don't stop me. Come with me," Nancy pleaded. She touched a wall switch, flooding the basement with light.

Reluctantly her father followed, but kept tight hold of her arm. Within seconds both the Drews began to sneeze. The place was damp and smelled quite moldy. The ghost was not in sight.

The Drews were amazed at the basement, which seemed to be a sunless greenhouse. Many rows of benches held pots of potting material, but no growth showed above the surface. Nancy poked a finger down into a pot and felt a tiny bulb.

"An orchid!" she exclaimed. "I guess the growers start these in the dark."

Mr. Drew sighed with a smile. "Nancy, I'm beginning to have second thoughts about buying Orchidiana for you. Even without the ghost to worry about, there's more to do here than I think you could manage."

Nancy chuckled softly, then suddenly turned serious. "Dad, let's go back upstairs. I want to examine that dark blue fluid. I have a hunch about it."

When they reached the front hall, Nancy began searching the floor for spots. Finding one, she wiped it up with her finger, smelled it, then transferred the sticky smear to a tissue from her pocket. "It's almost like glue," she said. "I guess it could be a sap mixed with blue dye of some kind."

Was this part of Mr. La Forge's secret formula?

Nancy decided to try to find out and bounded up the staircase. On the second floor she searched for the master bedroom, and identified it by initials on embroidered pillowcases on the bed. An old-fashioned desk with many pigeonholes and racks stood against one wall. It was open. Papers lay scattered on the top. The racks were filled with bottles, all containing fluid. Each one was numbered in sequence.

Nancy thought they must indicate a succession of experiments. She now noticed that in some of the low-numbered bottles the color had changed to a deep green. None held a true dark blue. Where had the tube the ghost used come from?

Bewildered, Nancy glanced around, and moments later her eyes detected a card on the desk which read FORMULA FOR BLUE. It was too complicated for her to memorize.

There must be a laboratory up here, the girl detective thought. Seeing the door to an adjoining room ajar, she pushed it open. A laboratory indeed! And a well-equipped one, it seemed. Its untidy appearance indicated that the lab had been used recently.

The ghost must have been at work, heard the visitors enter the house, and then used the ghost scare routine, which had failed to frighten off the callers. So the spectre had to escape in a hurry. Nancy was convinced by this time that the ghost was a live person playing the part. But who? And why? No doubt someone connected with the orchid secret.

On a hunch that the formula might be stolen, Nancy pulled her tiny high-speed camera from her pocket and quickly snapped photographs of the probably unfinished formula. Suddenly, she heard a noise behind her.

Turning, she was confronted by Hendricks. "What do you think you're doing?" he hissed at her, grabbing for the camera.

Nancy managed to hold on to it, quickly squeezed past him, and hurried down the stairs.

Her father met her. "Where have you been so long?" he asked her. "And who was that upstairs?"

She told him. The lawyer smiled. "I'm proud of you. The pictures of the formula could be very valuable for La Forge's children."

"Dad," Nancy whispered, "I think Hendricks is up to something. Do you?"

"Yes, but I'm not sure what."

Nancy pondered the mystery, and was suddenly struck with a thought. The ghost on the stairway had a very clear, pretty face.

"Dad," she said, "is any specific girl or woman connected with the La Forge mystery?"

The lawyer looked at his daughter intently. "Come to think of it, yes. Some of the estate money was left to Kiki's wife, who worked for La Forge as a secretary. It was a larger amount than was left to Hendricks, and he of course resented this. His wife didn't get a thing."

"I'll bet he was pretty angry," Nancy replied thoughtfully.

On a sudden hunch, Nancy went back upstairs to the lab. Hendricks was gone, and while searching the room for clues, she opened a desk drawer. Inside lay a white wig.

The ghost, Nancy thought, and picked it up. On the canvas lining was stamped the number "23L 109." In tiny letters against the "L" was "omax."

Nancy grinned. The wig had been rented or purchased at the Lomax Beauty Salon in River Heights! She replaced the wig and hurried downstairs to her father.

"Let's go, Dad!" she urged. "I have an errand in town."

It was not until they were in the car that she told him about the clue of the wig. They stopped at the Lomax shop and Nancy went in.

"You wish to make an appointment?" the woman at the desk asked.

"No, thank you," Nancy replied, "but I'd like to rent a wig like the one you gave to a young woman. Would you mind looking up your records? The number was 23L 109."

"This is most unusual," the woman said. "What is her name?"

"I don't know. I saw the wig backstage at a theater and looked inside."

The woman riffled through cards in a box and finally pulled one out. "This was a special order," she said. "If you want one, I'll have to make one up for you."

"How long would it take?" Nancy asked.

"A couple of weeks, but we have one to rent."

As Nancy thought about the mystery, she strained to catch a glimpse of the name on the card. What she saw was no surprise. In the upper righthand corner was written "Hendricks"! So his wife was indeed the ghost! She and her husband must be working as partners!

"I'll let you know about renting a wig like this one," Nancy said quickly and left the shop.

As the young detective rejoined her father, her mind was in a whirl. Then suddenly a new idea came to her.

"Dad," she said, "would you mind taking me home to get my car? I think I'll ask Bess and George to spend some time with me at the La Forge place. Okay?"

"As co-executor of the estate I can give you permission, but keep all your wits about you—and call me the minute there's any trouble."

When Nancy's close girlfriends received the invitation, George was eager to help solve the mystery of Orchidiana. But when Bess heard about the ghost, she was reluctant to go.

"You know I don't like even the mere mention of ghosts," she said, "real or otherwise!"

In the end, however, she agreed to go, rather than be called chicken. The girls went food shopping, then set off at five o'clock.

When they drove into the grounds of Orchidiana,

George could not resist teasing Nancy. "What a great place for you and Ned to settle down!"

Bess sighed. "I wouldn't live in a house with a ghost in it, even for free."

Once settled inside, the girls cooked their dinner and sat down to watch TV. Soon afterward, dusk turned to darkness. In a few minutes they heard a piercing screech.

Bess jumped in her chair. "What on earth was that?"

"Only a cat," George replied.

"I'll bet it's a black one," Bess said, always pessimistic.

Nancy flashed her strong lantern out the window, then laughed. "Only half your luck will be bad, Bess. The cat has pure white paws."

"You win again, Nancy," said Bess and sighed. "Just the same, I wish that cat would stop its horrible screeching."

George said to her cousin, "You might try throwing water on it. I've heard that's the thing to do."

Bess said no more and paid strict attention to the TV program until the three girls were startled by the sudden slamming of a front window shutter.

"That's funny," George remarked. "There's no wind tonight."

Nancy hurried to the window and gasped.

"What is it?" Bess asked nervously.

"The ghost!" Nancy replied.

George went to look. A figure with long white hair,

wearing a filmy, tiered, full-length white gown was dancing on the lawn. Every few seconds it would stop, make a bow, then continue as if an audience were demanding an encore.

"I must get closer," Nancy announced, squaring her shoulders, and ran outdoors. Bess and George watched from the window as their friend sped across the lawn after the dancer, who was running away from the young detective.

"Stop! Stop! I must talk to you!" Nancy cried out.

Instead of stopping, the dancing ghost ran faster. The chase led to the big greenhouse. The ghost rushed inside, slammed the door, and locked it.

Nancy raced to an adjoining shed, hurried through it and burst into the main building. The ghost was not in sight. Had she gone back to the house to change clothes?

Before leaving the greenhouse, the girl detective beamed her light under every bench and arbor. No one was in hiding. Nancy decided to go back to the house and search there for the elusive ghost. Again she was disappointed.

Oh, dear, she thought. Now what?

A sudden idea came to her. She retraced her steps to the room where she had seen the long, white-haired wig. The door was open, but no one was inside. Nancy went at once to the bureau and opened the top drawer. The wig lay inside. She felt it. Warm! It had been used recently.

At this moment a small woman walked in. She

wore a nightie and dressing gown. "What are you doing?" she asked. "And who are you? Let me guess. You're Nancy Drew, the snooping girl detective!"

Nancy did not answer. Instead she asked, "You're Mrs. Hendricks?"

"It's none of your business who I am. You don't belong here, so get out and stay out."

Nancy asked, "You don't own this house. It belongs to the La Forge estate."

The woman glared at her. "You think you know it all, but you'll never find out the real secret of the place!" she yelled.

Bess and George, wondering what had become of Nancy, heard the loud talking and came to investigate. By now the woman had shoved Nancy into the hall and locked herself in.

"Nancy, what happened?" Bess asked.

The girl detective put a finger to her lips and motioned for the girls to follow her along the hall. On the way she spotted a telephone on a table. Impulsively she picked it up, thinking she'd call her father.

As she held the receiver to her ear, a man's voice said, "Hi! Mrs. Hendricks?"

Nancy's mind raced. "Yes. Anything new?" she asked.

"Yes. Tell your husband I'm ready to meet his offer."

"That's good," Nancy said, trying to figure a way to get the man's name. She asked, "How do you spell your last name?"

"With a 'y.' Smythe. Ed Smythe in Eastville. And remember, no one can know about this."

"I'll remember," Nancy said, "and thank you."

As soon as the caller hung up, Nancy dialed her father at home and guardedly told him of the conversation. It was not until the next morning that she learned the real significance of the call. Mr. Drew drove out to the La Forge residence and told the girls that Ed Smythe was president of the Eastville Greenhouses, a large wholesale florist. He was a rival of La Forge's and La Forge would never sell the secret formula of the blue orchid.

Nancy asked, "You don't think Mr. Hendricks is selling the formula and intending to keep the money, do you? He doesn't even know the entire thing anyway. No one does!"

"It looks that way," the lawyer replied. "But your good detecting, Nancy, has foiled him if that's what he planned. I'll talk to Ed Smythe myself. In the meantime keep on with your work there. Hendricks might have figured out the remaining portion."

After he had left, Nancy decided on a bold move. "Let's go talk to Kiki," she suggested to the girls.

They found him in the workshop of the greenhouse unpacking a large box of pink orchids. "Oh, how beautiful!" Nancy exclaimed. "Where did they come from?"

"Hawaii," he replied. "My family grows them. When La Forge nurseries gets a big order, my folks send flowers to me."

Nancy looked at the young man and asked, "Kiki, have you ever mixed a formula to change the color of the flowers?"

"No, I never have, but I'd like to try—only I don't have the formula."

"I have part of it," Nancy said. "Shall we mix some of the sticky sap into the dark blue fluid and immerse the orchids' stems in it?"

"Let's go into the cold room," he said eagerly.

The cold room proved to be the NO ADMITTANCE room. Part of the space had been reserved for experimenting; test tubes hung in racks along the wall. Tools lay on benches. Buckets and empty glass bottles stood nearby.

"Where are the liquids?" Nancy asked.

Kiki opened a closet door. Inside were many shelves, all filled with liquids of various colors.

Nancy fumbled in her pocket for the paper on which the formula was written. She read it, then selected three bottles—red, blue, and one marked "sap." She poured a little of the two colors into a test tube and added water. Almost instantly a beautiful deep purple appeared. Nancy was disappointed.

"How am I ever going to get blue?" she said to Kiki, who merely shrugged and replied, "That's a pretty color."

Rather than waste it, Nancy poured the fluid into a bottle, added some sap, then put the stem of a white orchid into it. She and Kiki watched intently. Gradually the petals of the flower began to change, first to lavender, then deeper and deeper.

All this time Bess and George had been waiting in

the greenhouse and enjoying the orchid display. Suddenly Bess grabbed George's arm.

"Someone's coming!" she whispered, seeing a woman walk through the entrance door. "We should warn Nancy."

George raced toward the NO ADMITTANCE room. At the same time the woman started to run after her.

"You can't go in there!" she shouted at George.

George paid no attention. She threw open the door and warned Nancy and Kiki, who immediately stopped their testing. "Mrs. Hendricks," he muttered nervously. Quickly he closed and locked the door.

Mrs. Hendricks pushed George aside and tried to get in. Failing, she grew red in the face and screamed, "I'll fix you!"

On a nearby wall was a small red wheel with a sign above it: TEMPERATURE CONTROL. She turned the wheel to the mark for freezing. "That'll take care of unwanted visitors," she said with a sly smile to Bess and George. "Don't try to turn that off. It's automatic and will change itself in twelve hours and open the door—which is now locked from the outside!" She fled from the greenhouse.

Bess was in a panic. "Nancy'll freeze to death."

George jumped to the wheel. "I don't believe that horrible creature," she said. "Bess, pound on the door." At the same time she tried to turn the wheel back to NORMAL, but she couldn't find the button to unlock the wheel from its position. Minutes ticked by, and finally Bess, feeling blindly around a huge nearby switch panel, found the button on the underside.

The door opened. Nancy and Kiki staggered out, shivering, and were told what had happened. The two victims sighed in relief.

Kiki said, "Thanks for saving the priceless orchids in there."

"To say nothing of priceless *us!*" Nancy added.

Bess and George nodded. "But what are we going to do about that awful woman?" George asked finally.

"I have a plan," Nancy replied. "Right now we girls are going to leave here, but we're coming back secretly tonight." She led the way out of the greenhouse to her car. They climbed in and Nancy drove off.

"What's your big plan, Nancy?" Bess asked.

"To meet the ghost on her own ground."

As they rode into town, Nancy stopped at the Lomax Beauty Salon and went inside. She said she would rent the wig and paid the girl at the desk. After leaving Bess and George at their houses, she went to her own home and hurried to a bedroom closet. Nancy selected a pale pink bridesmaid's dress that she had once worn to an older friend's wedding.

She folded it carefully and put it in a suit box together with the long platinum blond wig from the beauty salon.

Directly after supper Nancy picked up Bess and George for the ride back to Orchidiana. Her friends begged for some details of Nancy's plan.

After hearing it, George asked, "How can you be

sure the greenhouse ghost will appear on the lawn?"

"If she doesn't," Nancy said, "you're to coax her outside so she will!"

Near dusk, Nancy put on her disguise and walked to the greenhouse. Bess and George watched from a window. Presently, the white-haired ghost came outside, carrying a vial of dark fluid. She danced across the grass, sprinkling the fluid as she went.

The figure flitted here and there apparently with no destination in mind. Nancy decided it was time for her to appear. She came from behind a bush where she was hiding. Imitating the other ghost, she danced gracefully toward the center of the lawn. Then she stopped suddenly, stretched her arms in front of her, and moaned loudly.

The other ghost turned. Seeing Nancy, she gave a cry and darted into the house. Bess and George rushed into the hall and blocked the stairway.

"Good evening, Mrs. Hendricks," George said.

And Bess added, "You dance very well."

A look of surprise and fear crossed the woman's face. "You—you know me?" she asked.

At this moment Nancy floated in through the front door. "Your game is up, Mrs. Hendricks," she said. "You and your husband almost got away with stealing the La Forge secret formula and selling it. Your ghost act was just to scare people off while you worked on figuring out the remaining portion of the formula . . . the formula you stole!"

"That's not true," the woman said. "Mr. La Forge gave it to us just before he died."

"I'm afraid you'll have to prove that in court," the girl detective said. Mrs. Hendricks paled.

They were suddenly interrupted by Kiki who rushed in. He stared in amazement at the two ghosts, but finally recognized Nancy.

He grabbed her hand excitedly. "I figured it out. Come and see!"

She followed him to the greenhouse where he pointed proudly to a beautiful dark blue orchid.

"How wonderful!" Nancy exclaimed. "How did you do it?" she asked.

"I can barely remember the combination of liquids I used," he replied excitedly. "But here. I wrote them down as I went along just in case I got the last part right!"

"You should be very proud of yourself." Nancy smiled warmly. "I'm sure the next owners of this place would be honored to keep you on!"

Kiki smiled. "I'd be honored too—on one condition—no more lawn parties and no more ghosts!"

NANCY DREW® MYSTERY STORIES By Carolyn Keene